It was around then I began to realize that there was some current between Chloe and me that was unlike anything I'd ever experienced before; it was a vague, clouded feeling that I couldn't quite place or identify. It didn't just happen all of a sudden; it was more like moments of dim awareness, followed by a gradual recognition that it was there without my understanding what it was. It's weird how sometimes things happen that you don't notice and then a long time afterward you see they were a part of something bigger, and you say, Oh, now I understand, now it fits. Well, that's how it was with this feeling. I know I felt it that night in Chloe's room, just for a moment.

HEY, DOLLFACE

DEBORAH HAUTZIG

Borzoi Sprinters
ALFRED A. KNOPF · NEW YORK

DR. M. JERRY WEISS, Distinguished Service Professor of Communications at Jersey City State College, is the educational consultant for Borzoi Sprinters. A past chair of the International Reading Association President's Advisory Committee on Intellectual Freedom, he travels frequently to give workshops on the use of trade books in schools.

For two of
my favorite people—
my mother and father

1

IT WAS a mild afternoon in mid-September. It had started off sunny, but the sky had turned steely neutral by the time I got off the crosstown bus and began walking to the strange school building on East End Avenue. I was going to the New Girls' Tea; the Garfield School for girls invited the new girls from each class the Thursday before school opened. I'd gotten the invitation from someone in my class who explained that two representatives from each class would be at the tea to greet everyone, and she was one of them.

The large double doors were locked, so I rang a bell

and waited. The doors were opened by a small woman dressed like a Victorian parlor maid, wearing a small black cap and a black-and-white uniform. I saw a bunch of girls standing in a group talking at the bottom of a huge staircase, and walked toward them. A large one came toward me.

"Hi. I'm Carolyn Smith."

"I'm Valerie Hoffman. You're the one that wrote me the letter inviting me," I said, as she checked off my name on a small blue pad.

"Yup, that was me!" She looked up and smiled, exposing her large, perfect white teeth. She was at least 5′ 10″, and I felt dumpy. At my old school I'd been one of the tallest girls in my class; I was 5′ 6″ and always liked being 5′ 6″; but now, as I looked around at the other girls, they all seemed taller, tanner, and healthy as horses.

"Well, we might as well go up now," said an older girl with long, stringy hair and buck teeth. "Are they all here?"

"All except one," said Carolyn, looking at her pad. "Chloe Fox."

"Chloe Fox?" I said.

The older girl glanced at me briefly and said to Carolyn, "Well, Mrs. O. wanted us up by three-fifteen."

Mrs. O., I thought. That must be Mrs. Olmsted, the headmistress.

"Mary will tell her where to go." I assumed Mary was the maid who had let me in, and we all began climbing the four endless flights of marble stairs to the upstairs gym.

"You can't use the elevator without a note from the nurse," Carolyn told me, and began chattering to another girl.

There were chairs set up in the gym, and we stood around a table eating cookies and drinking punch for a few minutes before we were told to be seated. One girl whose hair was obviously bleached approached me with a cheerleader smile.

"Hi. Are you a nine?"

"No, I'm a ten," I said apologetically.

"Oh," she said abruptly, dropping her smile. She turned and walked toward someone else at the other end of the table.

After a while we all sat down and adults filed in like a line of generals. All the girls stood up promptly as they entered the gym, and I hurried to get up with them, amazed that they were in such awe of authority. We listened to the president of the student body, the vice president of the student body, the presidents of the varsity team, student council, art club, glee club, French club, drama club, and then finally the headmistress and her assistant.

I kept turning around to see if anyone was arriving late; I wanted to see Chloe Fox. Once at my old school I'd heard there was going to be a new girl named Arabelle Kiss, and I couldn't wait to meet her because I liked the name. As it turned out, I couldn't stand Arabelle Kiss, but you never know. Nobody, however, arrived late.

Everyone left at around 5:00. I walked back to the bus stop alone, wondering why they were all so well mannered and athletic-looking; they almost looked like a different breed. I got off the bus and went straight home. We lived in a pre-war apartment building on Riverside Drive. It was a neighborhood, and I liked it. I'd never gone to school on the East Side before, but my friend Lori, who lived in my building, told me that all the girls who went to Garfield lived on Fifth or Park and never came to the West Side at all, or if they did it was by taxi or limousine. She went to school off Madison, so she knew.

Dad was in the living room reading music, and my brother Ben was sitting, dazed, in front of the TV in his room. Dad played the cello. When I was little I never thought playing cello for a living was anything special, but every time I told anyone, they said, "Really?" so I began announcing it with a sort of pride.

"So how was it?" he said.

"It was nice."

"Yeah?"

"Yeah. Everybody seemed nice. Oh, they said no one really checks the length of your skirt." We had to wear a uniform, something completely foreign to me, and according to regulations your skirt had to hit the floor when you knelt down. Mom, who never doubted for a moment that due punishment would be administered to me if we didn't follow the rules to the letter, had hemmed my skirt accordingly.

"I guess you didn't meet any of your teachers yet," said Dad, taking off his glasses and putting down his music.

"No."

"But you liked it. The girls seemed nice," he said, just to make sure.

"Well, I can't really tell yet. You should see the building. It's huge." I went into my room and changed clothes. "When's Mom coming home?" I yelled.

"Probably around nine-thirty," Dad yelled back.

"I thought visiting hours were over at eight," I said, coming back to the living room. My grandmother had been in the hospital for two months.

"They let her stay longer."

I sat down in the rocking chair. "So what's wrong with her?"

"They don't know yet—"

"They're taking tests," I finished for him. He nodded. "Bullshit. They've been taking tests for two months!" The phone rang and he jumped up to answer it. I knew he'd just give me the run-around, so I went to my brother's room.

"Hey, Ben." I sat down on the bed. "Hey! Boob! Dingding!"

He turned, surprised. "Oh! Val! You're home!"

"No kidding," I said sarcastically.

"Wanna watch TV with me?"

"Is that all you ever do? Why don't you ever read a book?"

"Oh, shut up," he said, turning back to watch a commercial. I felt better and leaned back to watch it with him.

I arrived at school early on Monday morning. Mom had gotten up to have breakfast with me, but I was a nervous wreck and couldn't even embark on the Carnation Instant Breakfast she kept telling me I needed. It made me sick just to look at it, so I left the house on an empty stomach. Mom kept telling me I'd faint if I didn't eat something and wishing me luck on my first day and asking me to call her at the hospital when I got home to tell her how it was.

I found my homeroom in a state of chaos. People were hugging each other, laughing and talking about their exotic vacations. I found a desk with my name on it and stood rather uncertainly. Several girls came up to me and introduced themselves; they asked where I'd gone to school before and a few other things, and then rushed off to talk to someone else. One girl, Patty, looked at the desk next to mine.

"Oh—your deskmate's Ginny."

I looked over at the label to confirm it. "Is she nice?"

"Yeah, she's nice. Her sister got her hand bitten off by a crocodile on a safari in Africa," she said grimly, securing her thin, mousy hair behind her ears.

"You're kidding!"

"No. But she doesn't want anyone to know. Now she has a fake hand."

"Does she go to Garfield?" I said incredulously.

"She graduated two years ago. Ginny has seven sisters."

"Wow," I said, duly impressed.

"Well, see you later."

"Yeah, see you," I answered, and she zipped over to

the door to say hello to someone who'd just come in. I wanted to find Chloe Fox's desk so I'd be able to spot her, but suddenly one of the seniors was at the door yelling, "Line up for prayers!"

"Prayers?" I said to nobody in particular. Prayers! I thought.

"Come on!" a tall Greek-looking girl said, brushing past me. I followed her. The entire upper school filed into an enormous auditorium. I looked down at my hiking boots and my green socks, green skirt and green blouse. Mom was right, I thought. I look like a tree.

It was a strange school. I went through my first week going to my classes, being utterly terrified by the gym teacher—I hated gym with a vengeance—and rushing home the second the bell rang at 3:15. I didn't sign up for any clubs. Everyone was nice, but no one really talked to me except Patty, which made me suspicious. I couldn't tell who stood where, who hung around with whom. Patty might be unpopular for some reason no one had made me wise to; why would she bother with me otherwise? So I just dashed home every day. Mom stayed late at the hospital every night. Half the time we ate what Mom had prepared cold, because Dad was never sure of how the oven actually worked—and a girl at school named Dora was without eyelashes from a recent oven accident, so I didn't try too hard either.

On Friday evening, I told Dad I wanted to go to the hospital. It was past 9:30 and Mom was still there. He said, "Val, maybe you shouldn't go. Grandma doesn't look like she used to."

"I just saw her last week," I said, a little annoyed. What did he think I was?

"She doesn't even look like she did last week."

I felt suddenly desperate.

"But suppose I never see her again?" I said, my voice rising. So I went.

My grandfather, mother and I were there when she died. Her teeth were out and a mask was over her face. A memory flashed through me of an afternoon when I was visiting Grandpa; he had gone to the bathroom to brush his teeth. I was very young then, and I called him for something, and he came out without his teeth in his mouth. I had screamed, "You're not my grandpa! He went out on the fire escape! You're not my grandpa!" I lifted my grandmother's hand and let go. It dropped. Suddenly I heard crying. Someone shepherded me out of the room; bright white lights had been flipped on over her bed. Mom and Grandpa came out and we stared at each other for a moment before we fell apart together in a tangle of arms and faces and lights and what sounded like sobs. It was us. "Forty-two years!" he kept crying.

The funeral was on Sunday. Death permeated the house. I don't know how they told Ben. I didn't want to know. I was sick of comforting people. Everyone kept telling me how terrific and supportive I was. As if I didn't need any support myself.

"You knew, Mom."

"Yes, I knew." We were sitting in the kitchen.

"You knew she was going to die!"

"We weren't sure—"

"You knew." She was going to cry again. "Why didn't you tell me?"

"I didn't want you to worry," she replied.

Then I began to cry. "Do you think wondering is easier?"

The house wasn't comfortable. Coming home was coming home to a house filled with people, people bringing food, bringing solace—some people I'd never seen before. And they all looked at me and kissed me and told me how much I'd grown and who I looked like, and tears welled in their eyes. I escaped to my room whenever I could, and sat like a zombie in my brown chair with the broken spring that I didn't want to have fixed, and did absolutely nothing. Sometimes I shook.

I skipped school on Monday. When I went in on Tuesday, I felt odder than I had the first week. I walked silently through the corridors and looked hard at all the girls that didn't see me. Nobody knew me. Nobody really knew I'd been absent. They don't know my grandmother died, I kept thinking. If one of their grandmothers had died it would matter to everyone. They don't know she won't be coming over with a shopping bag from Cake Masters with danishes and rye bread and even when I said it would make me fat she said *"fat?"* as though the very concept was ludicrous.

I saw Carolyn Smith during recess. She was standing alone eating an oatmeal cookie, so I went up to her and said, "You know what?" in a whisper.

"What?"

"My grandmother died."

"Uhh!" she exclaimed, looking horrified. She didn't seem to be able to say anything else, so I pretended I had to go someplace and went upstairs. The hall was empty. I saw my English teacher, Mrs. Corral, coming out of her classroom. She was old and really daffy but she didn't know it, and had a nose like Cyrano. I liked her and went over.

"Mrs. Corral?"

"Yes, Valerie!" She seemed pleased to see me.

"I'm sorry I couldn't hand in my paper yesterday. See, my grandmother died, and I had to stay home, you know. . . ."

She looked genuinely stricken. "Oh, Valerie, I'm so sorry."

"Oh, that's O.K. I just wanted to tell you—I'll hand it in tomorrow—"

"Don't worry about it, dear, don't worry about it—you just give it to me whenever you can." She put her hand on mine. It was an old hand, strong and covered with blue veins and with skin like egg membrane. "Oh, I'm terribly sorry, Valerie."

"Well . . . ," I said, because I couldn't say it was O.K. again because it wasn't O.K. at all. I believed she was sorry, and I felt dangerously near tears. I walked quickly toward the gym and downstairs to the locker room. It was deserted. I went into the bathroom and stood by the sink. Suddenly the door opened and another girl came in. She was skinny and her green skirt was droopy around the rear. She was wearing a black sweater, which was against the rules, and had long, wild dark hair and blue eyes like mine. She examined me quizzically.

"Hi," she finally said.

"Hi. Hey, you're in my gym class," I said, blinking quickly and trying to compose myself.

"Yeah, that's right," she said, smiling.

"Aren't you a new girl?"

"Uh-huh."

"Me too. I'm Val Hoffman."

"I'm Chloe Fox."

"*You're* Chloe Fox!" I said a little too loudly. "I wanted to meet you. I like your name."

"I hate it. But I was almost a Phoebe," she told me.

"I know a cat named Phoebe," I said thoughtfully. "I like Chloe better."

"So do I," she agreed. "Are you in Marese's French class?"

"Yeah." I grinned. "It's the dodo group. I'm terrible in French."

"So am I. They're moving me down."

"You'll like her. She's a sweet old lady. Hey—you're in my art class too. She's such an idiot." Chloe grimaced in agreement.

"I'm going to be a painter," she said. I lit up instantly.

"You *are*? So am I!" The bell rang for the end of recess. "What do you have now?"

"English. I hate it."

"I love English. I've got Math." We left and walked upstairs silently.

"Where do you live?" I asked.

"Riverdale."

"Riverdale? You come here every day from River-dale?"

She laughed. "See ya later."

"O.K.," I said, continuing up the stairs. I even skipped a few.

2

THE REST of that week was pretty depressing. Mom was sitting shivah at our house with Grandpa; it's a Jewish tradition, after someone dies. The mourners have to sit at home on wooden boxes or crates and people are in and out of the house all week, paying their respects. The idea is to make it easier on the mourners. I guess it's a good thing really, but it depressed me. Every day Mom would talk to me anxiously, asking if I was happy at school and had made any friends, and apologizing for not giving me enough attention. I told her not to worry, everything was great, and I'd gotten two people's phone numbers—Patty and Chloe. I didn't tell her I'd gotten the numbers from the office.

"After things settle down I want you to invite them over, Val," she said. I didn't have the heart to tell her to quit bugging me. She had the biggest and saddest eyes I'd ever seen, and she was always worrying. I wished so hard I could be happy just to make her feel better.

When shivah was over, Mom said we had to get back to normal. She looked like she'd been beaten from the inside. There was a big hole in the house; everyone knew it was there but tried not to look at it. Sometimes when the phone rang I'd expect it to be Grandma, but it wasn't. Or on Broadway, if I saw a woman from far away who walked the way she did, my stomach would do a double flip. But up close they were always strangers, and none of them had Grandma's dignity. I went with Mom when she had to sort through Grandma's things, and took a white handkerchief with little roses on it; it smelled just like her. She always wore *L'heure Bleu*. She had saved everything I'd ever given her, even the plastic rhinoceros I'd gotten at a penny arcade before I started kindergarten.

All that week after shivah, Mom and Dad were urging me to join some clubs. "Get involved in something," they told me every night at dinner. "There must be *something* you want to do. Join the art club, or write for the school paper," they coaxed. I just shrugged and muttered that I didn't want to, or maybe, which was the same.

Early one morning the next week, I was sitting on a back staircase at school, reading. I heard footsteps coming up and jumped, because I was cutting prayers. Chloe's face appeared just above the banister my foot was resting on, in between the bars. She looked up at me, relieved.

"We'd better not get caught," I said.

"I know, I know. At my old school, the nuns would send a note home to your parents if you did this."

"Nuns?"

"Yeah, I went to a Catholic school. I hated the nuns. They were tyrants. Once when I was in third grade—"

"You were there that long?" She nodded.

"Why?"

"My mother."

"So what happened?"

"Well, I had to go to the bathroom really badly, and Sister Lucille wouldn't let me go. I kept raising my hand but she didn't pay any attention, so I wet my pants in the middle of a Hail Mary." I laughed loudly, and she said, "I've never been so embarrassed in all my life. They had to mop it up and call my mother to bring me clean underwear."

"Do you like it here?"

"It's all right, I guess. Do you?"

"I feel like I'm on another planet," I burst out recklessly. "Everyone's rich and polite and I never talk to anybody and no one notices anyway. Well, Patty talks to me."

"Oh, Patty. What a twirp. All she does is gossip. But she's nice," she added.

"Yeah, she is nice. And that's a lot."

"I guess."

Actually I enjoyed hearing the gossip, and not knowing

anyone, I believed every word of it. "Do you really think this place is all right?" I asked.

"No. They're all debutantes."

I'd been hearing that a lot, and I wasn't exactly sure what being a debutante involved. "Listen, what's 'coming out'? Coming out of what?"

"Oh, when you're eighteen or so, if you're in the Junior League or your mother is on the committee or something, or your parents are rich or important, you go to all these dumb parties and you get an escort and you're presented."

"To what?"

"Society. The society crowd."

"Like saying, 'I'm available to anyone rich enough and proper enough'?"

"Sort of. Everyone at Garfield and Hopps and Briar gets invited to these Christmas balls and stuff. We can join anything we want if we go here."

"Oh, bravo. Just what I've been waiting for," I said. "Hey—your mother wouldn't make you do it, would she?" I asked suspiciously.

"Nah. She couldn't anyway. Those creeps! Forget it, kid."

"You know what? You know that girl in our class, Jacky somebody, the Greek one?"

"Uh-huh."

"I think she's beautiful."

"Yeah, in a way."

"Well, anyway, the other day I met her in the bathroom, and she was buying a *Kotex* from the machine."

"Yuck!"

"Yuck is right. So I told her I had a Tampax if she needed one, and she said—get this—her 'mummy' didn't 'permit' her to use Tampax."

"What?"

"Yeah!"

"Why?" Chloe said, her eyes wide and dancing.

"Exactly what I said. And do you know what she said? 'Mummy' wants her to marry a rich Greek yacht owner, and rich Greek yacht owners won't marry a girl with a busted hymen."

We were silent for a moment, contemplating this piece of outrage.

"But it can get busted anyway if you go horseback riding or something," said Chloe.

"I know. What can I tell you?"

A bell rang just then, and I remembered that we had art together first period. We leaped up and ran down the stairs, down the long corridor that led to the front part of the building and took the side stairway up to five, the top floor, where the art studio was, so we wouldn't run into everyone coming out of prayers. There was no one else in the room when we got there. One hideous, half-finished painting was leaning against one of the walls.

"Who did that?" I said.

"Rollins. She's not so bad."

"You *like* it?"

"No, I meant *she*'s not so bad."

"Someone told me she never takes a bath and the last time she washed her hair was in June."

Chloe laughed. "Her hair *is* really greasy."

"Where'd you get that sweater?"

"At a thrift shop."

"No kidding?" I was impressed.

"I went with Rollins last week." I felt betrayed. "She's pretty strange. I could never invite her home. Not that I'd want to. My mother would have a fit if I did, anyway."

"Why?"

"Ah, my mother's big on manners, and looking—you know—"

"Kempt?" I offered.

Chloe laughed. "Yeah. Rollins looks positively germy. I may look like a wreck, but at least I'm clean."

"My mother always liked my friends," I mused. "They're all at different schools now, though," I said, turning to look out the double windows at the brownstone roofs. "I probably won't see them much."

A few people began coming in, and we went and got two tables together.

"Uh—I was wondering—do you think maybe you could come over Friday after school?" I looked down and said quickly, "It's only cross-town, it isn't far. You could stay for dinner."

"Sure. Well, my mother doesn't like me taking the bus home too late, and she'd want to pick me up after work."

"That's O.K.," I said, relieved. "Or my dad could always drive you back."

"Oh, no, I wouldn't want him to do that."

"Oh, it's O.K.! He'd want to. He's really nice."

"I'll check with my mother." We looked at each other

nervously. "I can come over after school anyway, though. We get out early, so we'd have some time."

"Good," I said, and went to find a decent box of pastels. "I could call you tonight if you want."

"I'll give you my number."

"I got it from the office already." She looked surprised and then pleased.

"Then give me yours."

3

AFTER that we were fast friends. We were at each other's houses all the time, though mostly Chloe came to my house because it was easier than my going to Riverdale. Mom and Dad calmed down a little, though Mom still wanted me to invite some other people over too. Just to get her off my back I invited a huge girl named Eliza for lunch one Saturday, and when the time came for her to be picked up—*picked up*, imagine that— the buzzer was answered by Ben, who announced that Eliza's father was waiting downstairs. Eliza blushed deeply, and Mom and I looked at each other knowingly.

It wasn't her father; it was her chauffeur. Her embarrassment made me cringe, and after that I didn't bother with anyone else besides Chloe.

When Chloe finally did get moved into my French class it was the middle of October, and for the first time in my life I sat in the very front row, right under Marese's nose. It wasn't my idea; Chloe said if you sit in the front you never get called on, because they pick on the people in back who are trying to hide. She was right. Everyone else made fun of Marese, but we liked her. She always crossed herself and looked up at the ceiling when our responses were more outlandish than usual.

It didn't take us long to learn to sort out the girls at Garfield. There were basically two sets. One was composed of girls who never dreamed of doing anything without Mummy's and Daddy's approval, and they didn't approve of very much. These were the girls who went willingly to the Junior League Christmas balls with escorts who were sons of Mummy's and Daddy's friends, often from West Point, and who, like Jacky, didn't use Tampax because they always did what Mummy told them. Their families bought paintings as investments. These girls had chauffeurs, cooks, maids, nannies, villas, and tennis courts.

The second set was more worldly in the practical sense; while the Jackys had been to virtually every country in Europe and all the "in" islands, many had never been in a subway. These others had as much money and vacationing and such, but they knew how to lie and led their drinking, pot-partying existence with unblanched surfaces.

They were often given to ragged clothing, but it was a prop.

So Chloe was just about the only friend I had. Well, there was Lori, the girl in my building. I'd made friends with her when we were about eight. She had a Nazi father who was over seventy, a retired inventor who'd invented several flops that died soon after birth. He hated me for being Jewish and had three parakeets. Lori once had a canary that plucked itself to death. Her mother, a dyed blond in her forties who came from some obscure place in Eastern Europe and had affairs with rich shady men who took her on cruises, replaced the canary without telling Lori of its expiration, except that the new bird was blue. I remember Lori looking astonished and asking what had happened to Birdie (that was its name). Mrs. Frank had explained that she had brushed Birdie with a toothbrush to clean her feathers and they all fell out and grew in blue. We must have been very dumb; we believed it for at least six months.

I visited Lori a lot before Garfield. Her apartment was the creepiest place I've ever seen. It was dark and had dirty brown rugs, and in the living room there were two huge prints of Christ in Woolworth-gold frames, with fake candelabras, one on each side of each painting, like altars. There was a leopard skin on the couch and a 1961 copy of *Playboy* on the table, all of which gave the apartment an air of being a cross between a church and an illegal abortion clinic. It's amazing Lori turned out as well as she did. I used to go over there and listen to Lori recount her mother's or father's latest weirdness with relish. I also knew the life history of everyone in her class at school. Whenever I met one of them, I'd say something like, "Oh, yes, you're the one who was Joan of Arc in the school play and your brother broke his left foot roller-skating," and they were put off. I can see how it may have been unnerving. She went to a private school that had some strange philosophy based on that of someone named Rudolph Steiner, whom I'd never heard of and envisioned as being a space-y German who sat around all day doing strange body exercises. The Steiner kids all learned something called "eurythmics," which seemed to consist of telling a story by waving your arms around to help describe things, like the sun or rain. I found it all very suspicious.

But I didn't see much of Lori after I started Garfield. Lori was sensible and responsible and dependable; Chloe was always late and always lost things. When she liked an idea, she had an insane smile that would almost scare you if you didn't know her, and when she longed for something, she writhed and gasped a lot. She helped me make a papier-maché death mask, which we painted white with red trickling out of the eyes, and she was always taking pictures of me and leaving my head out of the frame because she liked the effect, which jostled my mother. Somehow we just fit. I tolerated every habit of hers that bothered me to distraction in other people.

I told Chloe about my grandmother. I thought it would be hard to explain about her dying, since Chloe never met her and didn't know me when she died; I thought maybe she wouldn't be able to feel what I was saying. But she did. It seemed like she always understood when I told her things. Like sometimes someone would say something and my feelings would be hurt; just some stupid thing no one else noticed, and if I told anyone else about it, even Mom, they'd say, "You're crazy!" But Chloe never said that. "People always tell me *I*'m too sensitive too," she'd groan. "I know how you feel." She always understood, and she never made me feel dumb or paranoid for letting things get to me. I knew we weren't crazy anyway; crazy people don't live in the world, they live in their own and just walk in ours. People use the word *crazy* all the time and don't know what they're talking about. They think being crazy is romantic and creative and wonderful, but I don't believe any of that. It was great having someone I didn't have to explain things to—Chloe just knew what I was talking about. We didn't just listen to each other; we heard each other too.

One December day I was on the East River Promenade, pants underneath my skirt. It was a study hall and the upper schoolers were allowed to leave the building during study halls and lunch, provided they didn't smoke cigarettes while in uniform and give Garfield a Bad Name. I was looking over at the factories. I never thought much about places I hadn't been, except that I might go there someday; when I listened to Baroque music sometimes I thought of courts and balls and chandeliers and how grand they must have been. There were sea gulls whipping around the sky like diapers, and I liked going out to watch them. There had been no one else out there when I went; then an old man came. He walked very slowly with a cane. He wore a greenish woolly coat, nice slacks and a hat and scarf. He slowly approached a bench. I kept watching him, waiting for him to sit down. He finally got to the bench and when he did, he reached into his pocket and took out a large plastic bag. I looked on, very curious as to what he would do. He slowly extracted a long white handkerchief, bent over and ran the handkerchief over the bench seat. After he was finished, he straightened and put the handkerchief away. He pivoted and very slowly walked away and out of sight. It made me feel weird—like I'd just observed a ritual and couldn't figure out what it meant.

I looked at my watch and dashed back to school for gym. Chloe wasn't there, and I knew she wasn't absent. It was basketball that day, and I threw the ball to the wrong team twice, thinking it was too bad Chloe wasn't there because she would have enjoyed watching me botch up, and wondering where she was. After I got dressed I was walking down the long corridor which led to the new wing of the building when Chloe came around the corner. She saw me and her lip began to tremble.

"Chloe! Hi, I've been looking for you, where were—" She burst into tears. "What's wrong?" She cried louder. "What happened?" She was hysterical. "Come on, come on," I said, dragging her into the bathroom at the end of the hall, pushing her in as I heard steps behind us.

"Chloe, will you please tell me what's wrong?"

She sat in the sink, crying and laughing. "My goddam zipper broke. I want to be an angel!"

"What?"

"I want to be an *angel*," she sobbed.

I didn't know what she was talking about, but that was Chloe all over again. I thought perhaps she just meant she wanted to fly away, but I didn't bother asking. The sight of her sitting in the sink in Garfield with her skirt all twisted around her jeans wailing that she wanted to be an angel was enough to make me want to say, "Me too!" But I just said, "Oh, my God. They've done it to you." She cried louder. "Don't let it get to you," I soothed, wondering what *it* was. "It's not worth it."

"I'm so sick of everything! I'm fed up! I hate these stupid prissy wasp teachers. I hate everyone here!" She gave a loud hiccup.

"Aw, Chloe, I know." She stood up and fell on me and hugged me. Then she sat back down in the sink and hiccuped again. I started laughing.

"My uncle Rudy died of the hiccups," I offered. "He really did. He hiccuped for three whole weeks before it got him." She sniffled.

"I don't know why I said I'd take pictures for that lousy alumni bulletin. I lost four rolls of film and that asshole Mrs. Beales *still* hasn't given me the shot she wanted in it and neither has Grimes and I'm going to miss the deadline and everyone's on my back and I had a fight with my mother," she said in one breath. "Oh,

Val—" she began to cry again. "*Why* can't I be an angel—" I didn't know what to say. "And I *hate* this uniform!" She tugged savagely at her skirt and the button popped off. She was wearing jeans underneath like I was and the skirt fell to her feet.

"Oh, God," she wailed.

I scrounged in my bag and produced a safety pin. "Chloe? Let's cut school tomorrow."

"Cut? But what about Lewis?" Our school nurse called you at home if you weren't in by nine, unless you called first.

"We leave the house—together. You sleep over. And we call in—separately—and we do whatever the hell we want," I explained, beginning to feel uneasy. Chloe was warming up.

"I've never—O.K. But not tomorrow. I can't sleep over tonight. Next Tuesday, and we'll do it Wednesday."

"What'll we do?" I mused. "I know. You can take me to a thrift shop, for one thing. I've never been, except to that crummy place we went to on Second."

"Yeah," she said, her mind off someplace else. "Don't worry, we'll think of stuff."

"I had a fight with my mother too. About my room being messy. Usually she just says, 'You're-a-walking-ty-phoon-I-can't-even-look-keep-your-door-shut-I'm-embarrassed-to-ask-Pearl-to-clean-it.' " Pearl was our housekeeper. Chloe was looking gloomily at the floor, so I continued. "But last night she started carrying on, about how I'd get bedbugs and how can I find my way to the dresser and all. Well, it's *my room*, right?" Chloe nodded. "What did you have a fight with your mother about?" There was a long pause.

"Well, my father, sort of."

"What?"

"I'll tell you later."

"Later? When later?"

"I'll call you. Oh, Val," she sighed, and took me by the arm. "Let's get out of here."

4

"SO TELL me," I said, carrying the phone over to my bed.

"Is it O.K. for me to call this late?" Chloe whispered.

"Sure. I'm just painting the door to my room. Wait till you see. It's got a big sun and roses and ivy and peach trees. I'm doing a constellation in silver. Got paint all over the rug." There was a long silence. "Chloe?"

"Shhh!" she hissed.

"What's wrong?"

"I thought my mother was listening at the door." I sighed; I was used to that.

"You are really neurotic, did you know that?"

"Wait a minute—O.K. Well, you know my father hasn't been feeling too well."

"What's the matter with him?"

"He had yellow fever when he was a kid and he has a weak heart. The doctor said he's supposed to take it easy, you know, not get excited."

"So?"

"So my mother was bitching out at him, as usual."

"About what?" I said, peeling paint from my fingernails.

"Oh, she was just nagging and bitching and complaining. She's been getting like that a lot lately, and he's so sweet, he just takes it. He's always nice to her. I can't stand it! He deserves better, you know?"

"Uh-huh."

"It just got me really upset, you know? So I started defending him. He told me not to, but I couldn't help it. So she started bitching at *me*, telling me I was always on his side, and I was a burden and I never help around the house, which is a lie, and I'd never get any place in life anyway and she was wasting all her money on me and why couldn't I be more like my sister."

"Then what?" I said in disbelief.

"Then I had hysterics and I started crying and screaming, 'You don't love me, you *never* loved me.' I really had a tantrum. They couldn't believe it."

"Wow," I said, at a loss. "But, Chloe, you know that isn't true."

"What, that she doesn't love me? Yeah, I know," she said uncertainly. "But maybe she's right, maybe I really am awful. She makes me sound like such a monster I start thinking maybe *I'm* crazy. Am I that bad?"

"You're the best!" I said angrily. "Boy, could I tell her off. Is she always like this?"

"Lately she's been bitchy all the time. But sometimes she's so nice, you wouldn't believe it's the same person. I feel so bad for my father."

"I know. But, Chloe, he's a grown man," I said confidently. "He knows her better than you probably ever will. He can take care of himself. So don't feel guilty about him."

"But he *can't*! He won't stand up to her!"

"Well," I said, thinking, that's his own affair, but it sounded too cold to say. I wanted to tell her she couldn't protect people from things. It doesn't work. So not to be miserable. It's so horrible when you think your parents are helpless. Instead I said, "I hate it when people throw that money business in your face. People who give you things and then never let you hear the end of it. I mean, if that's how they're going to be, who wants it?"

"I know!"

"I can't believe your mother said that. My parents would never even think it."

"Val. I've got to get off."

"O.K. Hey, what about next week?"

She giggled weakly. "How's tomorrow?"

I brightened. "Tomorrow night?"

"Would your mother mind my sleeping over?"

I groaned. "You jerk. She loves you. Besides, you're my one friend. She'll think it's *healthy* for me."

"Great. Gotta go. See ya in French."

"Argh. Chloe! There's a test tomorrow!"

"I know."

"Did you study?"

"Are you kidding?" she said.

"Me neither. I don't care. Well, sleep tight."

"O.K., dollface." She called me dollface a lot. Sometimes we called each other kid, but dollface was her favorite. Whenever she said it I had a flashing image of a white china doll with 1940-ish Joan Crawford lips and dark curly synthetic hair. I liked it, and when Chloe said it I usually gave her my favorite woebegone look and said, "Who'd buy *me*?" It was almost a routine. Chloe always answered with, "You're not for sale."

Friday morning we left the house at 8:30 and called in sick from a phone booth. Pleased with ourselves but still apprehensive, we scurried to the subway and took it down to Fourth Street. We were safe. Chloe grabbed my arm every five minutes and said, "This is great!" I think that morning was the first time I realized that I'd never had a physical friend before. My friends and I just didn't touch each other much, at least not on purpose or with feeling, and I had never really noticed that we didn't, till I met Chloe. She was always clutching me when she was scared or cold or happy, or if I was, and it was as though a door had been opened. A lot of people are so funny about touching each other; like it's a threat or something. When Chloe hooked her arm onto mine walking on the street, even I had these pangs of What-will-people-think, but then I'd think, this is New York, I'll probably never see them again, so who cares? Anyway, besides embarrassing me a little, it made me feel—well, warm, I guess. Like I was going someplace with my friend, and even if we weren't going anyplace special it was special because we were together. Even going noplace was great with Chloe.

Nothing was open yet and it was pretty cold out. Chloe lent me one of her gloves. We decided we'd buy a magazine and sit in Washington Square Park for a while. We chose *Vogue* because it made us both miserable to look at it and we couldn't wait to start examining each and every ad.

"I feel so silly being seen with this," I grumbled. "People will look and go, 'Tsk tsk, poor girl, it's hopeless.'"

Chloe groaned and threw her hands in the air. "*You*'re hopeless. Ha. What I'd give to look like you."

"You are off your nut, Chloe Fox. I've got big boobs and mashed-potato cheeks. You'd have to be insane to want to look like me."

"Your boobs are perfect, they're not big. And you've got beautiful skin and beautiful eyes and absolutely no hips and you're five feet, six inches. You're gorgeous," she said.

"Your eyes are nicer than mine and I'd give anything to be flat and so what if I'm five-six?" I countered.

"I'm five-four, *that*'s so what! And look at my poor tits! They sink *in*!"

I laughed. "At least you don't bounce around and jiggle when you run. Mine go flying around like superballs and all the New York bums make nasty cracks."

"I'll trade any day," she said.

"You look taller than five-four."

"Heels. Always."

I looked at her shoes. "How can you *walk*?" She shrugged.

"God, listen to us. Garfield girls, cutting school and buying *Vogue* like a couple of morons. I can't stand people who read *Vogue*," I said with disgust.

"Me either! Isn't this great?"

We sat huddled together on a bench and looked at every photograph, sighing over our unfortunate anatomical flaws, and pelting insults at all the plastic phony blonds. I made a mental list of my assets and then, tired of reducing myself to that, turned to Chloe and said, "Well, now, dear, and what's *your* value on the common market?" She gave me a sour glance and went back to the magazine.

Greenwich Village wakes up later than other parts of the city. When we couldn't feel our ears anymore, we began walking. Before we got to the thrift shop on West Broadway she'd told me about, we'd consumed several packages of gum and Chloe had a slice of pizza.

"My day off," she told me between bites. "I shouldn't eat this. Bad for my skin."

I'd never heard of thrift shops till I met Chloe. She taught me the whereabouts and price-haggling of wonderful dark places filled with furs, strange velvet dresses, hats, old jackets, tailcoats and feather boas. And millions of mismatched pajamas. We walked around all day, going into every pokey shop that caught our eye, finding twisted little streets we never knew existed and eating everything we felt like buying.

Chloe liked things I'd never considered before. She adored old pointy-toed spike-heeled shoes if they had a tacky ribbon or rhinestones adorning them. And those pointy glasses women used to wear. She'd pick up what I thought was an outrageous item and gasp, "Oh, I *have* to have this." I usually succeeded in talking her out of it; she told me she'd regret it. She said in a year they'd be the latest chic and I'd regret it too.

In the afternoon we went to a movie we'd both seen before and then we went over to a thrift shop on Mac-Dougal Street. After looking and digging into piles of clothing for a long time, and talking to the man who worked there, Chloe finally bought an old dress with a big rose pinned to it. I got a belt and a blue velvet blouse. I think it used to be part of a dress, but somebody cut it and hemmed it. When we left, clutching our big brown bags, it was beginning to get dark.

"Look at this—and it's only four-thirty!" Chloe exclaimed.

"It's winter," I reminded her. "I'm freezing." She took me by the arm. "I want to call my mother and tell her not to worry, O.K.? Then we can get some mocha."

"I don't know if I'll have enough money," she said, digging into her pocket.

"I'll pay. Hey—those were my pants, weren't they?"

"Mm-hm."

"They fit you a lot better."

"That's because I have big hips," she acknowledged mournfully. I called home from a booth, and then we went into a small, dark cafe with tables and chairs that didn't match. The furniture was Victorian-looking and too large for the place; some of the chairs had red velvet upholstery. There was an espresso machine making comforting noises behind the little counter near the entrance. We got the seats we wanted, by the window.

"I love it here," Chloe sighed, gazing outside and then back at me.

"Me too."

"Your mother's great," she said out of the blue.

"Yeah, I know. She's almost too great. I can't match it," I told her, feeling I'd said something important that she wouldn't hear.

"Well, kid, you're damned if you do and you're damned if you don't." She shrugged. "I wish my mother were more like yours."

"Yeah, but you'd feel guilty too. You're as screwy as I am. Chloe, am I strange?"

"Whaddya mean are you strange?"

"Last Passover I was at my relatives' house, you know? We all get together for holidays. When we got home, my mother said they all think I'm strange. So I said, 'They like me, don't they?' So she said, 'Well—they'd do anything for you!' " I made a face. "So I said, 'That's 'cause I'm *your daughter*.' "

The man came over to take our order. We both ordered mocha—coffee and hot cocoa with whipped cream.

"So anyway, she said, 'Of course, people love their relatives!' which is ridiculous, because I hate half of them. Except my mom went through the war, so I guess that changes things. So I said, 'Well, *I* don't. I can't stand blah blah blah,' you know. Are you bored?"

"With you?"

"So she said," I continued, " 'They think you're strange,' and I said, 'Why?' She said, 'Well—unconventional. Like Joey Moskowitz came up and kissed me. Did you kiss the Moskowitzes?' " I rolled my eyes. "I said, 'Of course I didn't. I see them once a year and I don't even know them and I don't know if I'd like them if I did! If I went around kissing everyone, what would kissing mean?' "

"You're not strange."

"Besides which, I don't have any friends, except for you."

"Well, neither do I," said Chloe.

"That doesn't make me feel any better!" She looked hurt. "Oh, I didn't mean it that way. I don't need them. I just meant I can't figure out why. If you ever left, forget it."

"I consider not having friends at Garfield a compliment," Chloe said pointedly.

"Mm, maybe."

The mocha came. It looked delicious.

"Val? You know, I saw a shrink for a few months."

I was dumbstruck. "When?"

"Eighth grade."

"Why?"

"My mother made me go."

"Why?"

She shrugged. "Oh, I was depressed a lot. These people at school told her I wasn't well adjusted."

I spooned some whipped cream thoughtfully. "Did it help?"

"No. He was an idiot, anyway. He thought he knew all the answers."

"Hm. Wow." This was a new idea to me. I always thought shrinks were *supposed* to know all the answers.

"Now I know anyone who *is* well adjusted at that place needs a shrink!" she added.

"I want to go to a shrink too, sometimes, but then I figure I don't need to. Maybe I just don't want to find out anything awful."

"Yeah," she said, not really listening.

"You know, Ben asked my mother if he could go to one."

"Ben?" she squealed. "He's in second grade!"

"Yeah, but a few of his friends go. Can you imagine? But Ben says this one kid who used to be impossible is getting a lot better. Ben wants to be either a shrink or a hockey player."

Chloe laughed. "Why a shrink?"

"He says he wants to hear all those crazy stories."

"I like your brother."

"Everybody likes him," I said with disdain. "I hate his guts. But I love him. He's a great kid." I knew it all fit together somehow. Chloe smiled, so I knew it was all right.

"What'd your mother tell him about seeing a shrink?"

"She told him when he was older and could pay for it

and if he still wanted to go, he could, but that she thought he could handle things pretty well right now. It's bad to ship your kids to a shrink the minute they have a hard time, they'll wind up basket cases if nobody trusts them to do anything themselves. Don't ya think?"

"Mmmm."

I turned and looked out the window. People scuttled by in herds, all hunched over and worried-looking. I sighed, glad that I was inside with Chloe and not in any hurry to leave.

"You know," I said, "it's incredible when you think how many people there are in the world. Like sometimes I think how every person is a soap opera, you know?"

"Yeah, and you always think your problems are just the worst, when there are millions of people probably thinking your problems are nothing compared to theirs!"

"I guess you've got to think you're important. Chloe—" I leaned forward. "When I get depressed I pretend someone's watching me on a hidden TV screen."

"Yeah? I do that too sometimes. I pretend I'm some mythical mysterious girl that everyone wonders about," she said, grinning darkly.

"Exactly. I guess I just like thinking someone's watching when I'm all—all alone; it makes being depressed glamorous instead of depressing, you know? And I don't mean God, who probably isn't there anyway." Chloe nodded. Not really believing in God was a recent development, and I hadn't told anyone how I felt, but then no one ever asked me one way or the other. I guess Mom and Dad just assumed that I knew God was there, but I wasn't sure anymore. When Grandma was alive and I went to temple with her I did, but figured I was so wicked and so beyond hope and there were so many rules I'd broken, I couldn't begin to get upset over it. Still, she had made me certain that there was a God; she was history, and tradition, and culture, she cried on the holidays, her very existence was proof that God was there and that being a Jew meant believing this. But after she died, temple was never the same again, and I began to wonder. What kind of a God would sit back and watch something like World War II and not do anything? And if he did watch it happen, why should I spend my time praying? I couldn't bring myself to care enough about someone I wasn't sure was there and wasn't willing to prove it; if God was there, He was just sitting back taking it all in so I never relied on His help in anything. If anything good or bad happens, I thought, people make it happen, not some God. I probably could have psyched myself into believing, but I thought people get lonely or desperate or awful things happen to them so they pray, thinking at least *someone* has time to listen and someone cares, and I didn't want to talk myself into being religious. Maybe one day I'll wake up believing, and that would be nice.

I came out of my daze and poured a packet of sugar into my mouth. "Hey, Chloe? What's your favorite color?"

"Dark blue, No, aqua. Well, actually, I don't have a favorite color, except to wear."

"Me neither. I love colors. I guess green and blue, if I had to pick. What's your favorite color to wear?"

"Black," she said without hesitation. I had never really worn black until I met her; she was always wearing black and I loved it, so I had started wearing it too. Whenever we met each other we looked ready for a funeral. I looked over at her and then down at myself. We were both in black shirts, black sweaters, and black corduroy pants.

"You look like a minister." I giggled.

She bowed her head and raised it, baring her teeth. "Confess! Confess!"

I gazed at her for a moment, struck by the energetic beauty of her face. Her lips looked as though they had lipstick on them, but they didn't; her cheeks were flushed, her eyes burned like blue gas jets, and her thick hair seemed to have a life of its own. "I'd like to paint you," I told her.

"Me?"

"Yes, you."

"Why?"

I rolled my eyes and shook my head, ignoring the question. "Maybe we should get going."

"O.K." She collected her cameras and bags and put on her enormous plaid coat while I paid. She must take hours undoing herself at night, I thought. You wouldn't know it to look at her because all four layers of shirts and sweaters were black, and it was hard to see exactly what she was wearing. She was carrying a big fishing-tackle bag, three cameras, several paper bags and her pockets bulged with rolls of film and Chapstick and keys and Kleenex.

We stepped outside into the darkness. The street was deserted.

"Val, what'd you tell Lewis you had?"

"A virus. That's what doctors always say when they don't know what the hell's wrong with you," I said, hopping off the curb and back up again. "Nice and vague. What about you?"

"Sore throat," she said, gagging.

"Are we terrible?"

"Nah." We walked to the park and sat down at the chess tables. A man came out of nowhere and asked us if we'd be interested in some acid. We said no thank you. He tipped his hat.

"Well, at least he was polite. Ben got mugged for a Yo-Yo last year, you know." Chloe laughed. "It isn't funny."

"It just sounded so pathetic," she apologized.

"You know that other new girl, Corrie Phillips?"

"Mm-hm."

"She takes Quaaludes. I didn't even know what they were."

"Well, Lucy *Jenks* gets stoned every day before school," Chloe said.

"You're kidding! I'm naïve, you know that? I thought she was just a complete blockhead, her mouth always hanging open and her eyes half shut and giggling at nothing all the time. How'd you know?"

"Everyone knows it. Val, I don't want to take that stupid bus."

"Come home with me," I offered.

"Can't."

I knew she couldn't be persuaded. I looked over toward the fountain at the scattered drunks. "Let's go." We got up. "Chloe, suppose we get raped?" I rasped.

"No problem," Chloe said offhandedly. "Nobody will rape us. We'll pretend we're gay," she said, and we elaborately put our arms around each other.

"Maybe some creep thinks it's kinky to rape lesbians," I whispered.

"We'll take our chances."

"Chloe, there's this cemetery down near Wall Street I've never been to. It's supposed to be really neat. You want to go with me sometime?"

"Oooh, sure. Next Saturday, maybe."

"Saturday—rats. I'm baby-sitting for Jason." I'd just begun baby-sitting regularly for Janet Elgin two nights a week, but she needed me that Saturday so I'd said yes.

"Well—another time, then."

"Sure." We got to Eighth Street.

"Val, I turn here."

"O.K.," I said, disengaging myself.

"Val? Will you always be my friend?" She looked frightened suddenly. I saw it in her eyes.

"Always.   Absolutely-positively-no-doubt-about-it-forever."

"Good," she said softly.

"Chloe? You know, Jason's father was acting funny the other night."

"How?"

"I'm not sure. I'll call you on Monday if anything happens."

"What, what?" she asked, wildly curious.

"He kept finding excuses to touch me."

"Where?"

"My hard-to-miss chest," I said, as she took in her breath and gave a long, low hoot.

"Pervert! How old is he?"

"Forty-five."

"Jesus, kid." She glanced at her watch. "Wow, it's late. I've got to go."

"Be careful."

"*Me*? Ha! You better keep me posted, dollface. I want to know every gory detail."

I waved and stood watching her run down the block till she rounded the corner, wondering if Dr. Elgin really was thinking of trying anything. Then I turned and ran to the subway as fast as I could.

5

I'D ONLY begun baby-sitting for the Elgins that fall. Janet Elgin was divorced, in her thirties and neat-looking. Jason, a mature eleven-year-old who claimed to have been a marijuana smoker since the age of six, spent Monday and Thursday afternoons and part of the evenings with his father. Janet somehow managed to arrange her social life in such a way that she had dates every Monday and Thursday, so I had a nice steady job right in the building. Dr. Elgin, who was in the midst of his third marriage with a baby on the way, would bring Jason home around 8:30, and I'd be waiting to take over.

The apartment fascinated me. In the living room there were bamboo screens draped with antique shawls and lace and Kate Greenaway-type hats with feathers, and two couches strewn with furs and oriental spreads. On the walls hung pressed flowers, framed, which Janet had collected. There were shelves filled with antique toys, and dozens of antique soldiers made of painted lead, and there were tiny pewter geese on the tables. There was a collection of colored glass mushrooms on another shelf near the window and I thought how nice they must look when the sun was setting. One night Jason took down a small laquered box from a high shelf and opened it for me, revealing a round glass eye.

The kitchen had a large butcher-block counter to sit at, and there were lots of spices and herbal teas in the cabinet. Vegetables hung in wire baskets, and there was a wooden salad bowl on top of the refrigerator with a constant supply of pretzels and sourballs. Janet's bedroom was off the kitchen, with lace drapes substituting for a door. She had a huge bed which took up most of the room, two tiny tables with open art-deco boxes overflowing with beads, and one small Tiffany lamp. Jason's room was in the back. He had a drafting table with small bottles of model paints lined neatly along the edge, a big electric train set, an aquarium which gave off a dreamy green glow and was filled with exotic-looking fish, a poster of Dracula, and a bed.

I really loved going there. I spent a lot of time looking through Janet's sketch books, which contained page after page of intricate ink drawings of flowers. But the last two times I'd gone, Dr. Elgin had behaved differently. He'd lingered after Jason had gone to bed, for one thing. And he looked at me differently. I'd had a pretty bad cough, and on Thursday he offered to listen to my chest. I let him thump around my back a little. I felt strange being around him that night; for some reason he made my heart race.

On Monday night, Jason went to bed and I was just getting up to make sure his lights were out. Dr. Elgin, who was sprawled on the other couch, put out his hand to stop me. I looked down at him. His hand was on my knee. He asked me if I'd bring him some water and I said of course. Then he ran his hand very slowly up my leg and said in this low, oozy voice, "You have nice legs." I was shocked when I saw where his hand was going and hurried off to the kitchen, saying, "Thank you," and blushing.

He said he wanted to make a phone call before he left. We sat across from each other as he talked. At first he just stared at me, and I couldn't help staring back. Then he pulled his chair in closer and our knees bumped suddenly. A squiggle of mysterious joy went racing through me like a hot-line. This, I thought, is terrible. Her lecherous ex running up her phone bill and dying to get his hands on me. He started playing with the shawl I was wearing. I always wore one of Janet's shawls when I went there. Then he held my hand tightly, and loosened his grip and tightened it over and over as his thumb swerved and drifted and created a whirlpool on my wrist. It was hypnotic. I sat, mesmerized, and then he hung up the phone and looked at me.

"You know," he said, "you have nice hands. They're small and cool. . . ."

"My mother says," I said slowly, "that shaking hands with me is like shaking hands with a dead fish." Plunk. Congratulations, Val!

"Well," he continued, undaunted, "you tell your mother that—no, don't tell your mother anything, or I won't ever do it again."

I smiled as seductively as I could and said, "Don't worry." He stood up and looked at my face.

"You know what?" he said, cupping my chin and tilting my head up.

"What?" I whispered, wondering what force it was that kept me from pulling away.

"You have a beautiful mouth." He placed three fingers on my lips and ran them back and forth. We walked over to the door and he turned and drew me to him, putting his arms around me.

I didn't know myself anymore and wondered where I'd gone; I felt like an onlooker, watching two strangers. I put my arms around him and let him hug me and rub his cheek against mine. It felt like sandpaper. Then he left, and I glided, stupefied, to the telephone to call Chloe.

"Well?" she said.

"Mm?"

"Oh, my God, what did he do?" she said breathlessly.

"He touched me."

"Where?"

"Um—let's see. My right leg, my left hand, and my lips," I told her. "Chloe, how come when he touched my hand it was so—incredible?"

"Is he good-looking?" she pressed, ignoring my question.

"He's the sexiest man I've ever seen. And he doesn't look any forty-five either. And you know what he did before he left?"

"Wait, wait, tell me from the beginning. Tell me *exactly* what happened," she ordered, and I did. When I finished, she said, "Wow. Val, this guy is sick."

"You mean, to want me?" I said defensively.

"No, you jerk. I mean, think about it! His son in the next room, his third wife—*third*—pregnant, and forty-five years old!"

It did sound pretty ghastly. "Yeah, he is, I guess." I thought for a moment and then said anxiously, "Chloe, how come I liked it? How come I let him? I didn't mean to let him, but suddenly there we were! He makes me feel like—like pudding. Oh, I don't know! Tell me!" I pleaded.

She just sighed. "When're you going next?"

"Thursday."

"*Oh, boy.*" She giggled.

"You're some comfort!"

"Listen, Val, don't let him sweep you off your feet," Chloe said. Then she said cautiously, "You—don't want him to, do you?"

"No-o," I said slowly. "I feel creepy about the whole thing. This isn't very wholesome, is it?" I laughed weakly. "Do you think he's damaged my frail soul forever?"

"No, but watch it. I've gotta go, kid."

"O.K. Christ," I said to myself.

"Oh, dollface—I told you you're irresistible!" she chided.

"Oh, sure. *Kiss* me dahling before we part," I swooned. I heard a noisy kiss and then the receiver rattling.

Thursday night, Dr. Elgin stayed to make phone calls again. I hadn't been listening to what he was saying, but I caught the last snatch of it. He was telling someone he'd bring her over some pills and said, "If you take these and smoke, you'll get high as a kite." I stared at him hard but he didn't seem to notice. I walked him to the door, and he stopped and turned to kiss me. I let him kiss me once. Afterward I remembered his remark on the phone and said jokingly,

"I didn't know you made house calls."

His expression became a slight smirk. "Well, you don't think you're the only one, do you?"

I looked away quickly, not knowing what to say. I wanted to yell, I'm not one at all. And then it dawned on me that I was angry. I looked back at him and thought, you royal creep, I can't stand you. Out loud, I just said good-bye.

I'd barely sat down on the couch when I heard keys grating in the lock. Janet came in. I had a dumb expression on my face; I could feel it. She gave me a strange look, and it occurred to me they must have passed each other. She leaned down and picked up the shawl which must have dropped from my shoulders while we kissed. First she asked me if I was taking drugs. I laughed and said of course not. *That*'s how out of it I look? I wondered. And then somehow she knew.

"Are you having an affair with Robert?"

I was horrified. "No!" Her eyes narrowed. "I've never —had an affair with anyone," I said, thinking: An affair is when you sleep with someone. Therefore this is not an affair.

"He's after you, isn't he? Yes, you're his type," she said, eyeing me critically as she sat down across from me.

"Well—" I hesitated. Me? Someone's type?

"Look. I don't care what you do with him, I really don't. But not here. Jason could get up at any moment."

"I know," I said apologetically, feeling guilty as hell.

"Listen, it's not your fault. My God," she said, more to herself than to me. "Well, yes, I do believe he would. That's just like him. With his son fifteen feet away. *Jesus.* I don't want Robert coming up here anymore." I felt almost relieved. "I'm going to tell him to send Jason up in the elevator alone."

"O.K. That's fine with me," I said. "I'm sorry. He's—"

"Yes, he's very persuasive." She nodded. "And very attractive."

"Yeah, he really is a killer," I said, marveling at our conversation.

"He'd be very bad for you."

51

"Yes. Yes, I know," I answered, realizing it as I said it. "You got me off the hook."

"Valerie, you don't need me or anyone to do that for you," she said flatly, and patted my arm as I left. "See you next week."

I let myself into our apartment quietly and took off my shoes. I heard Mom in the kitchen.

"Val?"

"Yeah."

"You're home early."

"Yeah. Janet came early," I said, feeling impatient. I had wanted to just go to my room and shut the door and brood.

"Mm, too bad. Didn't earn much tonight, huh?"

"Nope."

"Come sit with me in the kitchen while I fix something up for Daddy." I went into the kitchen and sat down on the washing machine. Mom looked like she'd been hit. She'd looked like that ever since Grandma died; like a light in her went out. Losing your mother must be the worst thing that could happen to anyone, I thought. She looked so defeated and sad I couldn't walk out on her. I pulled my feet up and wrapped my arms around my legs.

"Where's Ben?" I said.

"Asleep."

"When's Daddy coming home?"

"Around eleven." He was away a lot; he taught cello out of town and went on concert tours. "Oh, Valerie, did I tell you about Mrs. Dresner?" I perked up and smiled wickedly, glad to escape my thoughts. Mrs. Dresner lived way up on the fourteenth floor.

"No, what?"

"She accused Elmer of poisoning her groceries." Elmer was the doorman. I gave a whoop of laughter as Mom tried to suppress a smile. "Don't laugh. She's a poor, sick old lady. She must be eighty." She turned back to the stove. "When I asked Elmer about it, he said the latest is she turns up in the lobby at three in the morning all dressed with a pocketbook, saying she's going shopping. Elmer said, 'She's such a trial for the night doorman.' "

"And are the Johnsons still climbing through a secret doorway in her bedroom to spy on her?"

"Val, we're so unkind."

I nodded agreeably.

"Hey, Mom, I didn't tell you. You know what happened in the elevator the other day? Mrs. Dresner looked straight at me and said, 'Oh! Are you your father's daughter?' " I grinned as Mom looked on expectantly. "So I said, 'No!' and walked out of the elevator!" I feel better, I thought. That girl who was kissing Dr. Elgin, that wasn't me. Or was it? It must have been a part of me; a part of me *did* want to kiss him. I wonder how often Dr. Elgin has sex, I thought, kicking off my shoes. How often *do* married people have sex, I wondered. Once a day? Once a week? Once a month? How often do they want to have sex? I wonder how often Mom and Dad do it, I thought. Do they wait till the middle of the night when I'm asleep so I won't hear the bed creaking? Do they talk at all when they do it? I sat there working up the courage to ask Mom, and finally I said boldly, "Mom, how often do normal people have sex?" She looked ready to pass out. "I don't mean you or anything. I'm not asking about you. I just mean—people in general. Like people your age."

"There's no such thing as normal, Val," she said, and got up to rearrange some things on the shelf.

"Well, for goodness sakes, can't you give me a general answer? For all I know it's once a year! If I can't ask my own mother, who can I ask?" I bellowed, following her into the living room.

"I'm sorry, Val. You're right. I *want* you to ask me. I'm just not very good at discussing these things," she said weakly.

"That's O.K.," I said gently, waiting for an answer. Boy, and I thought *I'd* be uncomfortable. Here I am re-assuring *her*! "So?"

"Well—two or three times a week is normal."

"Two or three times a week? That's average?"

"Yes. I'd say twice a week is average." She jumped up and headed back toward the kitchen, and I followed her.

"But Mom, is it more for people in their twenties, maybe?"

"Yes, maybe it is. It depends on the people," she said. I hate putting her through this, I thought, but there it is. She's my mother, so I'm supposed to be able to ask her.

"Well, what about old people?"

"Not as much. It depends on the people. Some people have sex till they're very old, some don't."

"How come old people do it less? Don't they want to?"

"Most people, as they get older, don't want to as much as they did when they were younger."

"Why?"

"There's a hormone change." Oh, I thought. Menopause and all that.

"But some do?"

"I expect so." Well, I thought. I wonder if it's that nobody wants to do it with a woman who's saggy and droopy. Will no one want me once I start looking older and have midriff bulge? I saw Grandma once in the shower, and her breasts hung so low I couldn't believe it. It scared me at the time. Gosh, I hope I don't wind up like that; but I will. Shit. I wish I were flat, I thought, biting a fingernail absently.

"It isn't because no one wants you when you're all saggy, is it?"

Mom laughed a little. "Don't be silly. If two people love each other, that doesn't matter." She said it with such purity of conviction it sounded almost beautiful. She sounds so innocent, I thought. She'd only said what I used to think every married person felt, but lately every other movie and book was about people cheating on their husbands or wives or leaving them altogether and maybe Mom was the rarity. I wonder if what she said is true, I thought. Maybe it is. But why are looks so important now? People say they don't matter, but you could bet your life they were all that mattered at things like school dances. I wish they didn't matter; they shouldn't. People shouldn't care so much, they should look farther than that. But if I was a knockout, I told myself grimly, I wouldn't be ungrateful. Maybe Mom's just lucky. I always had these visions about how one day I'd meet *the* person and we'd just love each other completely and forever and go to museums and concerts and love doing the same things and that would be that. But maybe I won't meet *the* person. Maybe he doesn't even exist! No —he does exist, someplace. But suppose he's a Russian and we never even get to meet?

"Mom, do looks really matter?"

"No! Well, everyone should try to look their best, and that's about all you can do, but it's minor."

"No, Mom," I said thoughtfully. "How can someone know you're terrific and wonderful before they talk to you? They can't, right? So they have to like your looks before they decide to say hello, right?"

"Well, yes," said Mom, "I suppose that's true."

"So looks do count?" I pressed.

"Well, I told you, everyone should do the best they can with whatever God gave them." That sounded so simple, I began to wonder if she knew what people went through over their looks. Suppose God gave them acne or fat thighs?

"Mom, what about people who get nose jobs? And ear jobs? And God knows what else?"

"Well, I think that's all ridiculous," she said, obviously relieved to be off the topic of sex. "But if it makes someone feel better about themselves, it's worth it, I suppose."

"Well, didn't you once say that Shirley never would have gotten as far as she did in the fashion world if she didn't have her nose job?" Shirley was my cousin.

"That's the fashion world, Val. That's just the way it is in fashion. It's not what counts."

"But it counts for her!"

"In that way, maybe. But look at Shirley. She's not happy even with a nice nose."

"Maybe I should get a nose job." Mom looked at me as though I'd sprouted horns.

"Valerie, you're insane. You have a beautiful small nose. People pay thousands for noses like yours!"

"Well," I said lamely.

"What are you so worried about? You're a beautiful girl!"

"I am not beautiful. You'd say that anyway, even if I were hideous. I suppose it could be worse, though. But I wish I were flat-chested."

"Oh, Val, shut up, you're crazy. Women are *supposed* to have bosoms."

"Oh, yeah? Take a look at *Vogue*. Those women barely have bumps."

"Yes, and they eat nothing but lettuce and look like they're from concentration camps."

"They're supposed to be beautiful."

"They're ugly. They look like chickens. In Europe if someone said, 'You've gained weight,' it was a compliment."

"No kidding?" I marveled. That was a new one. "You

can get pretty hung up with all these ads and the clothes they're selling and stuff, you know."

"No, I don't know. Nobody wants a scarecrow," she said firmly.

"Oh, well," I sighed. "What's beautiful, anyway?"

"Beauty," she said, staring off like an oracle, "is in the eyes of the beholder. Remember that."

I rolled my eyes and said, "I guess I'll go do my homework." She came to suddenly and began rinsing some plates. Halfway back to my room I stopped. I wonder if she's ever been jealous or worried when Dad was away, I thought. I went back into the kitchen.

"Mom?"

"What?"

"Were you ever jealous?"

"Of what?"

I smiled. "Never mind." I went back to my room thinking, Nobody would believe me if I told them what a nice marriage my parents have. I'd trust Dad too. He always said Mom was the most beautiful woman in the world, even in the morning when she looked pasty and her hair was frazzled. They'd either say I was repressed and defensive or they just wouldn't believe it. Oh, well; I'll never get jaded, I said to myself as I flopped down on my bed.

A couple of days later Chloe and I were sitting in the library in between bookshelves, looking for some history book she needed. The three elevens who'd been loitering around the shelves whispering gave us a dirty look and slithered away, and Chloe thrust out her middle finger.

"I can't stand that class," she hissed.

"Hey, Chloe, those shoes Nelson was wearing—with the stripes—what are they?"

"*Gucci*, of course. And Cartier earrings. May they turn green."

I snorted. "Chloe, listen. What exactly is an orgasm?" She dropped the book she was holding.

"Shhh!" She put her hand over my mouth and looked over her shoulder to make sure no one was listening. I pushed her hand off.

"Well, I know what it is from the dictionary, but I don't know what it *is*," I said.

"Well, how should I know? What does the dictionary say?"

"Let's look it up." We hauled a dictionary over and looked. "Here it is. 'One. The physical and emotional sensation experienced at the culmination of a sexual act, as intercourse or masturbation, being a result of stimulation of the sexual organs, and typically followed in the male by ejaculation.' " She looked at me.

"Well, what's two?" she said.

" 'Two. An instance of experiencing this.' Now how the hell am I supposed to know what it's like from this definition?"

Chloe laughed. "Your expression. You're so cute."

"Well?"

"Well, I guess you have to have one to know, maybe."

"Well, suppose I've had one and didn't know it?"

"Nah, I asked my sister that once, and she said you

can't miss it." Julie was nearly twenty and away at college.

"How would she know?" I said.

"How do you think?"

"So we have to wait and see, then?"

"Yes, dear," she said mockingly.

"Rats. I can't imagine why it's so important," I said, feeling disgruntled.

"Me neither."

"You know, I had sex education in fifth grade and everything, but nobody ever bothers to tell you it's supposed to be fun. They just tell you it's for making babies," I grumbled. "I used to think, well, my parents did it at least twice."

"Live and learn, dollface."

I sighed and put the dictionary away.

"Hey, Chloe, did I tell you I asked my mother how often normal people have sex?"

Her mouth dropped open in amazement. "You asked your mother that?"

"Yeah. She said two or three times a week."

"Wow. You really asked her?"

"Well, I wanted to know. Who else could I ask? You?" Chloe gazed at me admiringly.

"Wow, dollface, you've got gall."

"Yeah, I know," I said with a satisfied sigh. "But give me credit—at least I didn't ask her what an orgasm was."

"Oh, my God," she said, laughing.

"Listen, kid, I've got to go downstairs. Hey! Christmas vacation starts next week!"

"Uh-huh."

"I take it you're not going to the Bahamas."

"Are you crazy?" she exclaimed.

"Possibly. Everyone else is going there, or some other place. We'll look like albinos. Where are the Bahamas, anyway?" She rolled her eyes. I never knew where anyplace was.

"I'll show you on a map sometime. Oh, Val—want to go to that cemetery over vacation sometime? And then maybe sleep over at my house?"

"Sure! Or you could sleep at my house if you want."

"I'm always sleeping at your house. Anyway, my mother doesn't want your mother to think she's unhospitable." We made a face at each other and laughed.

"Our crazy mothers. Well, I love your house, I'd rather sleep over there anyway for a change. I can see your tree." A bell rang again. "I've gotta go. Call me."

"Yup." I grabbed my bag, blew a kiss, and bounded out and down the stairs.

6

CHRISTMAS vacation started on a Thursday, and Christmas assembly was Thursday night. Chloe refused to go. I nearly backed out too, but Mom railroaded me into it. Parents were invited and she wanted to go, and was I ashamed of her? I felt so guilty when she said that, I put on my nicest dress and stockings and we walked to the bus stop in silence. It was freezing out but the air was still and brittle. My shoes felt strangely light as they clacked quickly along the sidewalk; I hadn't worn anything but hiking boots in months.

All the girls were dressed up and their hair was combed

neatly in place. Their parents looked angular and glittering. I felt very uncomfortable and wanted to run outside again. Instead I introduced Mom to a few people and then sat sullenly in a chair in the back waiting for it to begin. Once it did, I was glad I'd come. The glee club filed into the dark auditorium in long red robes holding candles, singing a song in Latin which I'd never heard before, in unison and right on key, clear and serene as a church choir. I sat back and closed my eyes, imagining I was in a chapel in the Swiss Alps. I opened my eyes and looked up at the girls on stage, still singing. They were all going away for vacation. I'm glad I'm not, I thought. I loved New York around Christmas time. It seemed like everywhere you went there were bells and holly and fake snow in all the windows, and sad-looking Santas with red noses and sunken chests, all looking like they needed a good drink. Near the Plaza the Hari Krishna people bobbed up and down in their sneakers chanting, their long pony tails flying. There were Salvation Army men playing trombones and trying to collect money, and canned Christmas music drifted out of stores. I always felt cheerful when I heard it. I gazed sleepily at the flowing red robes and three rows of faces. Noel. Feeling like a traitor, I glanced quickly at Mom. It had captured her too. Thanks for making me come, I thought, hoping she'd know so I wouldn't have to tell her and lose face. Chloe should have come. She was being dumb. You can hate the school but what's that got to do with this? I wondered if maybe Garfield wasn't so bad. I could just hear Chloe screeching heresy.

Chloe and I had saved the cemetery for Saturday, because I was going to sleep over that night. We met on Lexington Avenue and took the subway down to Wall Street. I was bundled into a linty pea jacket and millions of sweaters, and my head was mummified in a tremendous purple scarf, which Chloe said made my face look violet, like a cardiac patient. She was dressed in a black ski cap and an old golf jacket that used to be her father's, with even more sweaters than I had on underneath.

When we emerged from the subway station, we saw white. The first snowfall of the season. It was coming down in big dry wafers, and we childishly stuck out our tongues to catch some.

"Up in Massachusetts, where our house is, you can make snow cones with snow from the ground," I told Chloe.

"Mm. Clean snow." She breathed deeply.

Sometimes we went up to our house when Ben and I were on vacation in the winter, but some years we didn't because the roads were so bad. When we did, I could never sleep late. By 7:30 or 8:00 in the morning my room would be so light I'd wake up and pull up my shade, and the snow light that poured into my room was blinding. There was a white birch grove I could see from my window and the branches looked like glass.

Chloe and I stood still, looking down the deserted street. At the end was Trinity Church. We couldn't even make out the steeple tops in the swirling snow. We started walking toward it carefully, so that our feet wouldn't mess up the thin layer of snow too much.

"Val, could I come up to your house sometime?"

"Sure! Come for a weekend in spring when we start going again," I said.

"Can I? That would be great."

"I know a place we could go and paint where the view is beautiful. It's way up on a cliff everyone calls Crow Hill. You can see for miles and miles. Corn fields and churches and mountains. We can bring watercolors. You'll love it."

Chloe hopped up and down on one foot. "Val, I bet we're the only people here. This whole area is completely deserted." It was true. There weren't even any cars, and the silence sounded strange. We made our way to the cemetery and looked over the gate.

"Oh, Val, this is beautiful."

I nodded. It was a small graveyard on one side of the church. There was one large monument fenced in toward the back.

"I love cemeteries. You can just sit there as long as you want and no one bothers you."

"Yeah, you're not kidding," Chloe said with a grin. I grinned back.

"See that one?" I pointed. "That must be Alexander Hamilton's grave." We opened the latch and went in.

"Hey, Val, I brought a Polaroid."

"Really? Where'd you get it?"

"I borrowed it from my father."

"Did you tell him where you were going?"

"No. He wouldn't understand."

I ran up a small hill and lay down in front of a monument, folding my hands on my chest. "Chloe, take a picture, will you?"

She dropped her bag, ran after me with her camera and looked at me critically.

"You need a white camellia. And take off that stupid scarf." She squinted. "Get rid of the jacket, too."

"I'll die of exposure!"

"You will not. Anyway, if you do, I can just leave you here."

"Oh, all right," I said, unwinding my scarf and handing it to her. "Hey, get me a twig from that tree." She obeyed, and I took off my jacket and made a makeshift camellia with a twig and a white Kleenex. "Hurry up," I said, lying down again. After we got tired of taking pictures, we sat down and leaned on a stone.

"I miss my grandmother a lot sometimes," I said absently, thinking how depressing Hannukah had been without her. "You know, my grandfather's really lonely. He's over at our house all the time now." I loved my grandfather, but his behavior was beginning to get on my nerves. Mom sat with him nearly every evening in the living room and he wasn't the same. He was moody and actually sort of grouchy, which he never was before. He was always happy and never complained, and things that other people took for granted impressed him. The first time he had a strawberry-shortcake Good Humor he was in the park with me, and he just couldn't get over how good it was. He went to the circus every year and never told my grandmother: He thought the acrobats were wonderful. I thought to myself that Grandpa was the only person I knew who could enjoy almost everything. Even when someone turned on a television set, he would click his tongue and say how ingenious it was. And he was smart.

He'd been an engineer before World War II, and wealthy, but he lost everything. He even lost his wedding ring one day when he was hiding in a barn because he'd gotten so skinny it fell right off his finger. He told me how everyone thought he was dead because they found his dog tag, but he wasn't, and how he hid out in all these places disguised as a beggar.

"Well, maybe he'll remarry," Chloe suggested, interrupting my thoughts.

"Remarry?" I yelled. "Are you crazy? She just died!"

"Not now, but sometime maybe he will."

"No. Never. I wouldn't let him," I said, feeling ridiculous.

"Well," Chloe said. "It's awful to be alone when you're old." She was right, but I couldn't reconcile myself to the idea. We huddled closer together to keep warm, and looked straight up into the falling snow. "You know, we should live together when we get out of school. We could get a loft or something and fix it up and have room to paint."

"That would be incredible. We could have a fireplace and bird cages and big trees," I said dreamily. "And maybe a cat."

"With birds?"

"Oh, I wouldn't put birds in the cages. I just think they're beautiful."

"Mm."

We sat there for a while furnishing all the fantastic places we were going to live in, and finally I stood up and jumped up and down to try and unfreeze my feet.

"I'm petrified. Let's go in the church for a while to

warm up." We hobbled down the hill and out the gate and into the church. "That's one thing I like about churches. They're usually open. Temples are kept locked," I whispered, looking up at the ceilings in awe. There was one other person there, a woman up front, praying.

"Look at the windows, Val. Don't they look like smashed lollipops?" I gazed at the windows.

"I wouldn't mind living in a church, either," I said. After we warmed up, we went back outside and walked for a while, up and down empty streets, making our marks in the snow, which was still falling lightly.

"Now look, Val, don't forget what I told you. When we get home, don't say, 'Hello.' "

"What?"

"Say, 'Hello, *Mrs. Fox,*' O.K.?"

"Good grief," I said, making a face.

"It bugs her when you don't say, 'Hello, Mrs. Fox.' You always forget."

"O.K., O.K. Anything else?" I said peevishly.

"Don't curse."

"What?"

"Now don't play dumb. I've told you a hundred times she hates it when people curse. Not even *damn.*"

"But, Chloe, I don't even know I'm doing it half the time. I can't help it. I only curse when it's appropriate. I *learned* to curse from my *parents*," I added.

"Just don't, O.K.?"

"Look, if you're so afraid, I don't have to come. I've *only* been at your house about five hundred times. It's not as though I spout obscenities all the time."

Chloe looked exasperated. "Come on, Val, please? Don't be a martyr." She made a little pleading gesture.

I squinted at her indignantly for a moment and then sighed. "Oh, all right. I'll try to be good."

We went uptown and caught the Riverdale bus to her house. It was the fifth house on a paved, tree-lined road off the highway, big and white with green shutters and a huge tree in the front yard. We took off our shoes on the porch and went inside. I peeked into the kitchen. Mrs. Fox was standing at the sink, wearing a well-fitting dress and stockings and slippers. She always looked good; I'd never seen her looking the way you expect most people to look at home doing dishes. Her hair was dark and curly and cut short, and she had on a nice pair of earrings. She looked very businesslike as she rinsed a plate and put it in the dishwasher. Chloe took me by the arm and led me in.

"Well, hello, Valerie," Mrs. Fox said briskly, wiping her hands on a towel and giving the mandatory smile.

"Hello, Mrs. Fox," I said, looking over at Chloe quickly. She nodded approvingly.

"Hi, Mom," she said.

"Chloe, what's that jacket? I buy you all these nice clothes and you go around in the oldest rags you can find. I hope you didn't run into anyone." Mrs. Fox turned to me. "Why do *you* think kids insist on going out of their way to look disheveled?"

I gave a little smile. "Oh, I don't know. I guess we think we look good this way."

Mrs. Fox gave a noisy sigh and shrugged, muttering,

"I don't know. I buy her nice things and they sit in the closet." I tittered nervously.

After some small talk, Mr. Fox came out of the den beyond the kitchen. He was the kind of person you like immediately. He was very tall and thin and had high cheekbones and the same wide smile Chloe had. He said, "Hiya, Valerie! How've you been doing? Glad you could come!"

"So am I," I said.

"What did you girls do today?"

I looked at Chloe, my eyes questioning.

"We went to the Museum of Modern Art, Dad. There's a great Matisse exhibit," she said instantly.

"Yeah," I piped.

"Good. You kids should enjoy yourselves." He said it so good-naturedly I didn't mind being called a kid. He put his arm around Chloe. "How's my princess in her golf jacket?"

"Great." Chloe looked happy.

"You've never met our other daughter, have you? Julie!" She came in a moment later. "This one's home from the old grind. Work them to the bone out there." He winked. Julie looked a little like Chloe, but her hair was short and she wasn't as skinny or as flat-chested. She seemed nice.

We stayed in the kitchen for a few minutes, and then Chloe and I went to her room, which I loved. The walls were painted lavender and the ceiling was white. She had a large Vuillard print on one wall and a Picasso on another, and a little table by the windows with three avocado plants. There was a bed unit with two beds up against adjacent walls. There was a table in the corner joining them which had a stereo on it, and one of the beds could be rolled under the table to save space.

I sat on the floor as Chloe pulled a huge carton out of her closet filled with clothes; it was her reject box where she put things she was tired of wearing, and whenever I was over I could take whatever I liked, provided I'd return it if she ever wanted it back. Chloe had a strange habit of cutting all the collars off her shirts, because she didn't like collars. She also cut off sleeves if they were short-sleeved shirts; she hated short sleeves.

I whimpered at the sight of the demolished Bonwit Teller shirts. "How *could* you?"

She grinned helplessly.

We went through her clothes until dinner, which we all had in the den, where the Christmas tree was standing, dripping tinsel and crazy-looking angels and Tucan birds Chloe had made out of dough and then painted. Mr. and Mrs. Fox asked me about what my parents were doing and about school. Whenever I began to loosen up, Chloe kicked me under the table, and I was glad to get back to her room after helping her do the dishes.

"I'm a very polite person, you know," I said when we closed the door to her room. "No one ever complained about me *before*."

"Well no one is now either."

"Hrmph," I said sulkily. Then she reached under her bed, pulled out a big box and opened it. "What's in there?" I said, leaning over to look.

"This," she said, "is my beautiful-lady collection." I peered in and saw a pile of cut-out pictures of women.

"Did you get those from magazines?"

"Yup."

"What for?"

"For my beautiful-lady collage. I had this brainstorm one night last week at three in the morning. See, I have this theory. See this?" She picked out one of them and showed it to me. It was a brunette model, very pretty, wearing a low-cut black cocktail dress.

"She's pretty," I said, waiting for an explanation.

"Yeah, she's pretty. But she's not *different*. I mean, if you go down to Bergdorf's or something, you see hundreds of women like that."

"Not that pretty."

"But if you saw them from the back, or even from the front, really quickly, you wouldn't be able to tell them apart if you saw them again."

"I know what you mean. I have a cousin who had a nose job, and she's pretty, but she's pretty like everyone's pretty. I always think I see her across the street or something, and it isn't her."

"Right. Well, I'm collecting these pictures, see, until I have a whole box of them, and then I'm making a big collage out of them. And someplace on the collage I'll have a picture of you and a picture of me. And we'll be the most beautiful women on the whole collage."

"We will?" I said doubtfully.

"You bet your ass we will. You'll see. I'm going to paste the cutouts overlapping and everything, so you won't really be able to see anything but parts of these," she said, pointing to the box. "You know, a face here, a leg there, half a face, a breast. Like that. But we'll be in there all the way. Maybe I'll blow up that picture I took of you in the park."

"You're using naked women too?"

"Sure. They're exploited, so I'll exploit them even more, like saying big deal, it's a breast. Half the world has two apiece."

"Can I take the picture of you?"

"I want you to," Chloe said, going back to the bed and pulling out a pile of magazines. "Want to help me cut out some more?"

"Sure." We sat around going through magazines and cutting. Chloe turned on the radio.

"Chloe, I love it here. I feel safe."

"Thanks, kid."

"Your house is so beautiful. You're rich," I said accusingly.

"I am not!"

"You must be. Look at this place."

"This is nothing compared to what those jerks at school have. Your apartment is just as nice."

"But both your parents are lawyers, aren't they?"

"So?"

"So lawyers are rich."

"They are not. Anyway they have a lot of expenses, and after taxes they're really not rich."

"Oh, phooey," I grumbled. "Everyone says 'After-Taxes-I'm-Poor.' I don't believe it." Then a fast song came on the stereo. "I love this song," I said, tapping my feet. Chloe got up and danced around the room, and I got up with her, feeling giddy. After a while I got tired and flopped on the bed to watch her.

I don't think I ever said how beautiful Chloe was. But beautiful like no one else. It wasn't only that she had beautiful teeth that never needed braces, and gorgeous eyes, sometimes a very light gray and other times an astonishing, intense blue, and thick hair that would have been long ringlets if she hadn't forced it into mere waves; she had something else, something I can't explain very well. There was a kind of passion about her, which always made me think of her as a zooming screaming vision, always exciting and never bored or boring. Sometimes I'd look at her face and wonder if she knew how beautiful she was; I told her occasionally, but she said I was crazy, and that I was the beautiful one.

"Chloe?"

"What?" she said, landing on the bed and grabbing a magazine and scissors.

"I saw Dr. Elgin on Broadway the other day."

"You *did*? You didn't tell me! What'd he say?"

"Just hello. And he smiled. Chloe?"

"Mm?"

I hesitated. "The other night my father came home and he hugged me and I felt funny." She didn't react. "You don't know what I mean, do you?" She shook her head no. I picked up a scrap of paper and fiddled with it. "Well. I mean, look at Dr. Elgin. He's nearly my father's age and he's all over me. I mean—my body—" I waved my arms around. "*Men* want it." She nodded. "When I hugged my father I thought, My God, he's a man too. I never thought about my parents having sex, not *really* thought about it. I can't imagine it. So—so I got scared, you know?" She looked up from her magazine. "It just made me think that the only reason my father isn't attracted to me is because he won't permit himself to think that way."

"Well, he's normal," she said simply, after a moment.

"Yeah, but I mean, it isn't *innate* or anything. If he didn't know who I was, who knows? If he wasn't married to my mom, that is," I added quickly, listening to my thoughts uneasily. "It's just scary to think about it. I got scared when he hugged me. Not scared of him, but—" I felt flustered, not knowing if I was saying it right. "I tried to think of him objectively, just as a man, but I absolutely couldn't. It's impossible. I don't know if I'd like his body, or what." I shivered.

"I've never really thought about it," said Chloe, putting down her scissors. "My dad's just my dad."

"So is mine. But he's a man too. Isn't that weird? I never thought of him as a *man* before! Chloe, I never used to think about things like this. Is something wrong with me?" I was shocked to feel a tear rolling down my cheek. "I get so mixed up sometimes. Things get complicated," I said, wiping it off and feeling another start down my other cheek. Chloe picked up a corner of the bedspread and gently dabbed my face.

"Whatsa matter, dollface?"

"Oh, I don't know." I leaned my head and rested it on her knee. "Am I too terrible for you?"

"Val, you're the greatest," she said, and pushed the hair out of my eyes. I shut them for a moment and then lifted my head to look at her. It was around then I began to realize that there was some current between Chloe and me that was unlike anything I'd ever experienced before; it was a vague, clouded feeling that I couldn't quite place or identify. It didn't just happen all of a sudden; it was more like moments of dim awareness, followed by a gradual recognition that it was there without my understanding what it was. I never said anything, thinking, What would I say?

I don't mean to make this sound like a big thing, because it wasn't, not then; in fact, I hardly even noticed it, and if I had told anyone about Chloe at the time I'd never have mentioned it because it wouldn't have occurred to me. It's weird how sometimes things happen that you don't notice and then a long time afterward you see they were part of something bigger, and you say, Oh, now I understand, now it fits. Well, that's how it was with this feeling. I know I felt it that night in Chloe's room, just for a moment, like when there's a fly buzzing in your room and you can't see it but then the buzzing stops and you forget. A chill came over me and I jumped up abruptly to switch radio stations.

We sat around listening to music, talking and cutting up magazines until late, and after having some corn flakes in the kitchen with Julie we went upstairs to the attic where Chloe painted. There was a bedroom up there too, with a big double bed, where Julie slept, and the other room was strewn with tubes of paint, rags, and canvases. I made Chloe show me some of her old paintings, ones I'd never seen before, and I looked at each one for a long time. Chloe didn't paint the way I did; I painted a lot in watercolor, which I liked much better than oils or even acrylics. My paintings were light and impressionistic and had an underwater quality, as if I were afraid to make a definite statement. Hers were clear and dark with harsh lines and strange people, and I was struck by their power.

"Chloe, these are terrific," I said, putting down one that she'd painted on cardboard.

"No, they're not. They're lousy."

"I wish I could paint like this."

"You're crazy. I love the way you paint."

"Oh, why argue?" I said. "I really love your work. Can't you just believe me?"

"O.K., I believe you. Thanks. But you're crazy." We talked to Julie for a while about Garfield, because she'd gone there too, and then we went downstairs to bed.

"I wish we could sleep upstairs," I whispered. "Then we could make noise." Her parents' bedroom was across the hall from hers.

"Next time, when Julie's back at school."

"O.K.," I said, and put on the pajamas Chloe lent me. I pulled the top on quickly, because I hated getting undressed in front of people. "I dread the day I'll have to strip for a guy," I said glumly. "Maybe I could hide under the sheets." Chloe flipped off the light and turned on the radio very softly.

"What about Dr. Elgin?" she teased. "Would you hide under the sheets from him?"

"Hell, I'd hide in the closet," I said, pulling the blankets up to my chin. We whispered for about ten minutes and then I must have fallen asleep to the soft drumbeat coming from the stereo above me.

7

BY THE time Christmas vacation was over I was almost glad to go back to school, though I'd never have admitted it. I was getting tired of reading and watching the Million Dollar Movie. Chloe and I ran around the city a lot, but after a while we'd been every place we wanted to go and kept winding up at the Metropolitan Museum just to get in out of the cold. Everyone at school had great suntans, just as we had predicted; Jacky had gone all the way to Greece for hers. Patty was the only one who hadn't gone away; she got her sunburn, she told me gravely, from sitting under a sun lamp, and she burned her boobs too and was excused from gym because she couldn't wear a bra and it hurt when she bounced.

One Friday, Mom and Dad and Ben and Grandpa all drove up to Pennsylvania to visit some cousins. They were going to spend the night and asked me if I wanted to come but I said, No, Chloe was going to sleep over. I could have told her I had to go away, but the prospect of having the whole apartment to ourselves was too good to pass up. It's not as though we wanted to do anything like smoke that we wouldn't do when everyone was home; it was just this terrific feeling of freedom. Usually when she came over we'd hole up in my room with the door shut, but Dad would be stomping around the house or practicing, and Ben would have a friend over and they'd be making noise in the living room, and Mom would be trying to write and grumbling at everyone to shut up, and even with my door shut I felt like I was at Grand Central— *plus* I felt conspicuous for having my door shut in the midst of all that ruckus. I was really glad to get rid of everyone for one night.

Chloe and I snuck out of school early by way of a back door in the new wing, which had a big sign on it saying USE ONLY IN CASE OF FIRE. "Don't worry," Chloe assured me. "The alarm isn't turned on." We opened the heavy black steel door and the fire alarm went off. I thought I'd have a heart attack; Chloe grabbed my scarf, nearly choking me, and we bolted out the door like cats and raced up to York Avenue, turning the corner to safety. No one ever did find out it was us.

We walked downtown congratulating each other and

spent the afternoon roaming up and down Fifty-seventh Street. All the card-and-candy shops were selling the last of their chocolate Santa Clauses at half price, and I bought a few for myself. Chloe said chocolate made her break out. We walked all the way west, past Tiffany's and Berg-dorf Goodman's, which we told each other probably had its summer clothes on the racks already. As soon as the big Christmas rush was over all the winter stuff was reduced like crazy and you felt like a jerk for having paid a lot for it, plus you felt frantically under-equipped for the next season. Department stores always made me feel like I never had enough. We peered into the Russian Tea Room and promised each other to have lunch there someday. "We'll get really decked out and order martinis," Chloe said, and I nodded approvingly. I took Chloe to my favorite art-supply store and introduced her to Sam, one of the men who worked there. He knew me from when I went to the Art Students League on Saturdays. We hung around there for a while, looking and talking, and then crossed the street to pick up a catalog at the Art Students League.

Mom had left us enough food for a wedding reception, and Chloe spent ages with her head stuck in the refrigera-tor, deciding what she wanted. We ended up taking every-thing out and putting it on the table, and settled into the big green kitchen chairs. Kitchens are really the best places to sit and talk in.

"Dig in," I said happily, as Chloe swallowed a piece of chicken. "Hey, you know, Patty's been running around saying she thinks she's pregnant."

"Oh, phooey. She's a virgin."

"How do you know?"

"Because," Chloe said patiently, as though talking to a child, "the ones who do it don't run around yapping about it."

"Oh," I said lamely. "Who does it?"

"Oh, Rollins does, probably, and North."

"How do you know?" I persisted.

"*Boy*, you're a pest! I just *know*. I know the kind of guys they run around with."

"Wow." I couldn't imagine either one of them having sex with anyone. "Isn't that kind of young?"

She nodded, and started on her second roll.

"Can I put on your green shirt? Mine's too hot," Chloe said.

"It's right there. On the washing machine," I said, as she went to get it. "Hey, Chloe? I read an article the other day. About how women are afraid to even kiss each other in public nowadays because they're afraid everyone'll think they're gay."

"Yeah?" she said, smiling slightly.

"Yeah."

"That's stupid. People should do what they feel like doing, as long as it doesn't hurt anybody." She pulled off her shirt, her back turned to me. I looked at her thoughtfully. What's she thinking about? I wondered. Is she saying it's O.K. to be gay? Or that it's stupid to worry whether people think you're gay when you're not anyway? I remembered reading in *The Diary of Anne Frank* about how Anne wanted to feel another girl's breasts and offered to let the other girl feel hers, but the other girl didn't want to. I guess if you're cooped up all that time and miss out on everything you start doing with boys when you get to be the age Anne Frank was, it's O.K., I thought. She had an excuse to want to do it, anyway. But what about people who don't have any excuse—they just want to? Do I want to? Is it sick to even think about? I wonder what Chloe looks like from the front, I thought, watching her put on my shirt. She never undresses in front of me. Does she undress in front of other girls?

"But if someone's gay it hurts people," I said suddenly.

"Who?"

"Their parents."

"Yeah, that's true," Chloe said, sitting back down at the table. "But you can't get married or sleep with someone you don't want to sleep with just so your parents don't get upset." She began to laugh.

"What's funny?"

"Well, I was just thinking about gay people living together. Their parents are probably so happy 'cause their sons and daughters aren't living in sin. If they only knew!"

I laughed too.

"Do you think homosexuality is a sin?" I said.

"I don't know. I mean, I don't *feel* like it's a sin. I really don't know."

"I know what you mean. I don't *feel* like it is either. But . . . ." Chloe nodded knowingly. I didn't really know what I thought of homosexuality. When I was a kid I couldn't understand it at all, and when I asked Mom about it she never really answered me. She'd just get embarrassed and mumble something about "pretending to be married." So when I saw gay couples on the street I'd think, Oh, she couldn't get a guy, or he couldn't get a girl, so one of them must be pretending to be the opposite sex. It was second best, sort of. But it was beginning to occur to me that maybe it wasn't that way at all. It's so hard to know what to think, I brooded. It used to be there was a right and a wrong. If I told someone I thought homosexuality was a sin, then I'd be lying. But if I said it was perfectly O.K. I'd feel weird, because I wasn't sure about that either. When I thought of gay people having sex it seemed really strange. But then, any sex seemed a little strange! There are some things, I thought, that I'm just too young to understand.

After we finished eating and put away all the food and washed the dishes, we went into the living room and collapsed on the floor. Chloe and I never really *did* anything when we visited each other, except sometimes we cut up magazines for her collage. But usually we just sat around talking. I guess to some people that's boring, but we never got bored.

"Chloe, I wanted to tell you something." I paused significantly. "I've thought about it a lot and I've decided we should become gypsies."

"Gypsies!" she chortled, crunching into an apple.

That's what I like about her, I thought. She never laughs at ideas like that the way the friends at my old school probably would, and she doesn't act like they're impossible, either.

"Yeah," I said. "We'd run away. To Europe, you

know? France, maybe, or Scotland. Where's Appleby?"

"England."

"There's a gypsy fair at Appleby every year. I read about it in *National Geographic*. We could go to that and join a band of gypsies. God, Chloe, it would be incredible. We'd run on the moors and have red cheeks and be really healthy like in those old Hayley Mills movies, and ride stallions and cook meat over a fire on a long stick, like shish kebobs, you know?" She nodded, her eyes gleaming. "And we'd smudge dirt on our faces and there'd be a fiddler—and we'd dance—" He'd play in minor keys only, I thought to myself, and we'd get up and start dancing like mad in the firelight, hair streaking, and no stopping. I could picture Chloe there perfectly.

"Suppose no band would take us?" Chloe said, as though we were packed and ready to go. "Couldn't we just be our own band?"

"Sure we could. We could do absolutely positively anything. But I'd want to go to Appleby first. So we'd know more, you know? And decide after. Here, I'll show you the pictures." I got the magazine from under my bed and brought it in. There were pictures of gypsies sitting around fires at night in front of bow-top wagons, and lying in sunny green and lavender fields near wagons painted in passionate circus colors. Even the wheel spokes and brake shoes were covered with intricate designs in gold and royal blue and crimson.

"Look, it says a gypsy will sell anything he owns," I said, pointing at a caption.

"That's because he's free, he's not tied down by anything and doesn't care about *having* things," Chloe said firmly. "When I go away for even a weekend it takes me three hours to pack. I hate feeling like I need *things*. We should run away and not even bring a suitcase. Do they *live* in those wagons?"

"Yeah," I said dreamily, flipping a page. "You know, I heard someplace that gypsies used to steal gold and make their kid swallow it, and then wait for the kid to crap it out."

"Hey, that's smart!" Chloe remarked. She got up and sank into the couch, and I sat down next to her. "We could have the best time, just going wherever we felt like going and staying as long as we wanted." She was silent for a moment. Suddenly she turned to me and said softly, "Would you really run away with me?"

"Absolutely-positively-no-doubt-about-it. I wouldn't run away with anyone else ever."

"When?"

I squinted, thinking. Chloe flopped her head like a rag doll and nestled against my shoulder, slipping her arm under mine. My muscles tensed.

"We'll do it," I said, feeling her breath on my neck and burying my face in her hair. It smelled like vanilla. "Unless you poop out on me. We'll do it."

"Mm," she murmured. "Me? Poop out on you? Hey, dollface, would I do that?" I barely felt her lips tremble as each word vibrated gently against my neck. I looked down at her face, half hidden behind masses of hair; her eyes were closed. I sat absolutely still in the strange, sweet freeze that had taken over my body. It was the feel-

86

ing I'd had that night at her house, but stronger, and it didn't go away. My eyes scanned the room unseeingly; I was only aware of Chloe's face resting against me, and the chills that ran up and down my arms each time she exhaled quiet little puffs of sleep.

When I was sure she wouldn't wake up, I placed her head back on a pillow carefully and switched off the light. I got a big blanket from the linen closet and covered Chloe with it. Where should I sleep? I thought. I stood uncertainly for a moment, and then took off my jeans and crawled under the blanket facing the other way.

I couldn't fall asleep, though. After fifteen minutes of lying in the dark, I got up and took one of Mom's cigarettes from the coffee table. I sat in the middle of the room and lit it, letting it burn, watching Chloe sleep through spirals of blue smoke. After ten minutes I climbed back under the blanket and went to sleep.

8

I GUESS that's about when I started having the daydreams about Chloe and me. I'd always been big on daydreaming; I'd decide who I wanted to think about, and conjure up scenes with them, doing and saying all sorts of things I didn't have the courage to really do. In the ones with Chloe we'd be lying around someplace talking, and I'd get upset about something, and Chloe would run her fingers over my face and say "Whatsa matter, dollface?" Then she'd fold her arms around me and rest her head on my shoulder. Or sometimes I'd be sitting in a chair and she'd be playing with my hair, and it felt terrific. Anyway, in all of them we'd be physically close. I really didn't know why I liked making up scenes like that in my head, what it was about Chloe that made being held or having my hair fixed different, or why those scenes held the strange allure they did. I don't think I thought of it as being sexual attraction until later, or if I did I wouldn't admit it to myself. I guess I thought I wasn't capable of really having *that* sort of feeling; I couldn't imagine anyone I knew feeling that way, and the people who did were aliens to me, living in another world entirely. They weren't regular people like I was, they were people you raised your eyebrows about. I wanted to tell Chloe about my daydreams but somehow I kept losing my nerve, thinking how strange they'd sound if I said them out loud. I'll have to bring it up accidentally-on-purpose, I told myself. Just to test Chloe's reaction. So I'll know if I'm weird or something.

School was really dragging again by the end of February; it always did, every year since I could remember. February was such a rotten month; spring vacation seemed ages away, and even when they switched Lincoln's birthday around to give us a long weekend it was depressing. The streets were full of gray slush and streaked with dog shit. Winter always seemed like a letdown after Christmas, and especially after New Year's with Guy Lombardo making you want to cry or just bury yourself till the season was over. By March I was bored to death and counted the days till Easter break.

One night about a week before vacation I was baby-sitting for some new people in the building. There were two kids, Mark and Helga, and the father owned a funeral parlor. I guess there's good money in that, because their apartment was really ritzy and they always overpaid me. I think people blow a lot of money on funerals when they don't want to, so no one will think they're cheap. After the kids were in bed I dialed Chloe's number.

"Hello?" she said jauntily.

"Hi, it's me. Watcha doin'?"

"*French*. Can you believe it? I've been waiting for an excuse to stop."

"I'm baby-sitting. For the funeral-parlor people. Chloe, they've got enough tranquilizers in the bathroom cabinet to kill off every neurotic on the West Side."

"You looked?" she said gleefully.

"Yeah. One of my less admirable habits. The best way to find out about people is to check out their books and medicine cabinets."

"And refrigerators," she added. "Boy, I'd never hire you."

"Oh, me neither," I chuckled. "I wouldn't want anyone checking out *my* things."

She laughed. "Val, you're amazing."

"Not at all. Just unscrupulous. Listen, Chloe, we're going up to Massachusetts as soon as vacation starts, just for a few days. Can you come?"

"Yeah! Oh, when's Easter? I have to be home for Easter."

"Not till after. We'll be back in time."

"I'll go tell my mother right now."

"O.K., I've got to go anyway. I can't wait."

"Me neither. Bye-bye, dollface." Clink.

Chloe arrived the day we were leaving with three overnight bags.

"What's in all those?" I said incredulously.

"Oh, my paints and pads and rags and stuff. And some clothes. Do I need more than one sweater?"

"Yes."

"Good. I packed four."

"Aw, Chloe, you could have worn mine!"

She shrugged sheepishly. It was a long drive up, and we had dinner at a diner on the way. Chloe and I sat with Ben and a few bags in the back seat, squashed over to one side. Chloe leaned against me, and I leaned against the car door, my cheek pressed against the cold window. I thought about my daydreams, which I still hadn't told her about. How come if it were Ben leaning on me I'd push him away, but with Chloe I actually like it? It was like that on the bus sometimes; if some fat smelly slob leaned against me I got mad, but if some cute guy did it I liked it and hoped he was doing it on purpose. But what about Chloe?

When we got there it was late and Chloe and I rummaged through the garage for a while, claiming everything Mom wanted to send off to Hadassah. We told her she might as well give it to us and eliminate the middleman, since we went to the Hadassah thrift shop on Third Avenue anyway. She seemed to think it was funny and wound up giving in, and after we'd collected everything we wanted, we went to bed.

The area where our house was is really beautiful. We had lots of land and trees and a lake. Summers got kind of dull, because there was absolutely nothing to do, especially if you couldn't drive, but for painting and reading it was perfect. At the beginning of every summer I went on a Thoreau kick and by August I went loony and never wanted to read or paint again, but when we started going up in the spring I fell in love with the place all over again. I fell asleep praying for good weather, so Chloe and I could paint.

I heard a faint tapping and mumbled, "Mm? Mm, yeah, c'mon in." I was tangled up in my enormous flannel nightshirt.

Chloe stood beside my bed. "Good morning," she sang. "It's beautiful out. Your mother says it'll go up to *seventy*!"

"God, what time is it?" I struggled to turn over. "Seventy! Wow."

"Ten-thirty." She sat down next to me.

"I feel like a newborn kitten. I can't open my eyes."

"Well, hurry up and get dressed. Your mom's making breakfast. I'll be downstairs, O.K.?"

"Yeah, yeah. Get me out of here." She took my arm and hauled me out of bed, and I stumbled into the bathroom.

When I got downstairs Mom and Dad and Chloe were on the porch.

"Where's Ben?" I asked, not displeased.

"Watching—"

"TV," I joined in. "Why ask?"

"You were no better at his age, darling daughter," Dad said, reaching for a roll.

"I was too, and you know it."

"Don't be mean to Ben. He's so cute!" Chloe said. I shot her a dirty look. I can't stand it when people tell me how cute Ben is. I know perfectly well he's cute and I guess I'm glad he's not gross or anything, but my own best friend defending him in front of my parents!

"You watched 'Captain Greenjeans' every morning before school," Dad continued.

"Kanga*roo*. At least I did intelligent things in addition. I *read*."

"She did, Victor." Mom nodded, coming in with a plate heaped with cheeses.

"Wow," Chloe said, gazing at the plate puddle-eyed.

"I suppose I should urge him more," Mom said, wrinkling her eyebrows into an anxious furrow.

"Yeah. You don't make him eat the way you used to make me eat either, Mom," I said accusingly.

"Well, maybe it's better this way. So he'll be calm and easygoing. Someone once said you should have your second children first."

"Hrmph," I grumbled. So I was their guinea pig. Oh, well.

"Chloe, take more," Mom ordered, pointing at the different plates of food and going to the kitchen for more.

"Dad, will you drive us up to Crow Hill?"

"Sure," he said. "I have to buy milk—we need milk, right, honey?"

"Yes," Mom called from the kitchen. "And margarine, and—"

"Make me a list," Dad said, looking flustered.

"For two things you need a list?" I said.

"What?"

"Never mind." I shook my head, giggling.

Chloe and I hurried to finish eating, and then gathered pads, pencils, camera, Kleenex, transistor radio, paints and brushes, and stuffed it all into canvas bags. I went and filled a shopping bag with food and several jars of water to add to the collection, and we piled it into the car. We drove up to the end of our road, turned and began going up a winding, unpaved one.

"Here, Dad—stop here." I looked out the window of the car. Trees. A steep hill. And there was the stump I always looked for to remind myself where to start climbing. Chloe and I got out of the car, and agreed that Dad would come around four o'clock to get us.

We entered the woods. It was dark and chilly and churchlike. I looked up and saw beams of light streaming through the patches of new leaves. The hill was so steep that we were practically crawling part of the way. We finally came to a flat clearing.

"Over this way," I said breathlessly. "If this stupid shopping bag tears I'll have a fit."

We kept walking, and then the woods ended abruptly. We were there. A huge area of solid white and gray rock, in three levels, each about four feet below the other. We put down our bags to look; we were above everything, a rolling panorama spread before us. There were tiny houses and long wheat-colored fields and white steeples, and the cloudless, perfect sky which was that special blue you see on the first spectacular spring day, when everything looks freshly washed and colors seem brighter and you see things you never noticed before. We jumped down and looked over the edge of the bottom level. It was a steep drop, and a lot of the trees were still bare, but here and there a shimmer of leaves glinted like green cellophane in the sun. The only sounds were crickets and the wind; it seemed almost *un*natural compared to the constant undercurrent of traffic sounds in New York. It makes you want to write idiotic, corny poetry, I thought.

"This must be incredible in the fall," Chloe whispered. She scrunched up her face and gave a little scream. "Val, I'm so glad I'm here with you!"

"Me too." We stood for a while just looking at the view, and then I plopped down and pulled out the radio. "Classical?"

"Yeah."

I found WQXR. They were playing Corelli. We picked spots and took our things out of the bags. Chloe was one level lower than I was; we didn't like sitting together when we painted.

"Do you have an extra pencil?" she called. "I can't find any." I tossed one down to her, and began to sketch lightly on my watercolor block.

We painted, hopping back and forth a few times, and finished our first ones in an hour. We looked at both paintings. I thought they looked great together; it was obviously the same view, but the paintings were completely different.

"Yours is so much better," Chloe whined.

"Oh, shush." I sat down next to her pile and crossed my legs. "Listen, Chloe, will you go to that dance with me they're having at Collegiate the week we go back?" Collegiate was a boys' school.

"No way."

"Aw, how come?"

"How come? I'll tell you how come. Because it'll be the same as last time and the time before that. We'll spend three hours deciding which jeans to wear and then nobody'll even notice we're there."

I had to admit she was probably right. It was amazing how long it took to pick the right jeans. And then whenever I left after hours of deliberating, Mom would say, "You're going to a dance like *that*? How can you dance in those *shoes*?" I don't know what she thought dances were like.

"Chloe, there's always hope, isn't there?" I said timidly. "They can't *all* be creeps."

"Yeah, well, if any of them aren't, they stay at home. Anyway, I hope for bigger and better things than some stoned Collegiate asshole thinking he's doing me some big favor by asking me my name."

It's funny, I thought, when I go to dances to meet boys, I hardly ever have a good time. If someone says hello or dances with me once it's a big deal, like Chloe said. But compared to the things Chloe and I did together it seemed kind of degrading. Like it was O.K. to settle for having a lousy time with someone just 'cause he's a guy. But still I wanted to go to dances! When I get to college I'll meet all the intelligent ones, I thought. Like Mom's friends. The men she knew were terrific people. I wonder if they were all creeps in high school too, I pondered. Or maybe they're not creeps, they're just scared. This was an incredible thought. Scared of me? Why would they be scared of me? Oh, ugh. I just meet the wrong ones.

"Well, I'm not going if you're not," I said, a little disappointed. I picked up a pebble and tossed it over the edge of the cliff.

"Don't worry, dollface. You *know* what it'll be like. Stick with me. Let Patty and all those other morons knock themselves out."

"O.K., O.K.," I said glumly.

"Hey, Rodney asked me out again," Chloe said brightly. Rodney was the pimply, rich brother of a friend of Julie's. He was always asking Chloe to go out with him and once in a while she gave in.

"Are you going?"

"Yeah. He's taking me out to dinner."

"You're mean. You don't even like him."

"Oh, he's not so bad. He's actually sort of nice when he's not acting like Mr. Know-It-All. He can't help the way he looks. And he always takes me to great places."

"Well, see? At least you've got old Rodney. You should come to the dumb dances and find *me* some faithful ugly nice guy."

Chloe laughed. We lay down then and dozed off for a

while, and when we got up Chloe wanted me to take some pictures of her. She posed, brushing her hair back dramatically.

"Do I look like a Renoir?" she queried.

I eyed her critically. "Nope. Those women were built like dairy cows."

"Thanks!" she said sarcastically, and pouted, crossing her arms over her chest. I pouted back at her and we both laughed. Chloe leaned her chin on her hands. "Val, I wish my parents would get divorced."

"What?" I said, aghast.

"Well, I do."

"Listen to her," I said to an invisible audience. "Entire books are written about miserable kids learning to cope with broken homes and trying to get their parents back together, and she's wishing her parents would get divorced." I couldn't imagine anyone wishing something like that. I remembered when I was little how scared I got whenever Mom and Dad had a fight. I'd go to Mom and say, "You're not getting divorced, are you?" and she'd laugh and say, "Of course not!" I worried about it anyway and always felt relieved when they made up.

"If they did, I'd live with my father," Chloe was saying. "We'd get a neat little apartment in the City so I could see you all the time. I wouldn't have to worry about taking that stupid bus."

"Do you think they ever would get divorced?"

She got up and walked to the edge of the cliff and sat down, dangling her feet. "No. One time I thought they were going to separate. They didn't, though."

"Chloe, I bet they love each other." I went over and

sat beside her. "Really. I bet they do. You never know about people, even if you live with them and you think you know them." I thought of times when I'd catch Mom and Dad looking at each other in a funny way or talking about stuff they did before I was born, and it made me think, There are whole sections of them I'll never know, no matter how old I get. "Chloe, it's true," I said, as she stared off silently. "I used to think I knew my mom better than anyone did, even my father. But there are some things I'll never know about her that he does. I'll bet your parents love each other deep down. Maybe I'm naïve."

She looked at me gratefully. "Maybe you're right. It's just so hard sometimes. I mean, my mother's so irritable, and my father just listens to her. I think my mother resents having to work, you know. I think she thinks she should be able to sit back and have things given to her."

"Yeah, I noticed that. She's got nerve, expecting your father to pay for everything."

"But she's under a lot of pressure too, you know. With a job and two kids and all," Chloe said.

This was the first time I'd heard her defend her mother. "Yeah, she is," I agreed hurriedly. "Anyway, just 'cause people act a certain way doesn't mean they feel that way. I'm always bitching at Ben, but I don't hate him." She turned to me and took my wrist in her hand, squeezing it. Chills ran up and down my back.

"You're better than a shrink, kid. You know, I've never talked to anyone the way I talk to you."

"Me neither," I said quietly. I should tell her about my daydreams now, I thought nervously. I tell her everything else. Why can't I tell her this? Would she tell me? Our heads were so close I could see the pores on her nose. We stared at each other in silence for a long time. What's she thinking about? I wondered. Does she touch me just like she'd touch anyone else? No, it can't be in my head, I thought, remembering the night we slept on the couch. She didn't fall asleep on me the way she did by accident. No other girl had ever fallen asleep leaning on me the way Chloe did. What would she think if she knew I'd been having weird daydreams about her? Or that I'd thought of touching her? Would she be disgusted, or would she want me to? Suddenly we heard sounds coming from far away: Dad's car horn. We both jumped, the moment gone. Then we threw our things into our bags, and began a half-run through the woods and down toward the road.

We came back to New York three days later. We were going to stay another day but the weather turned chilly and damp, and Mom had to get back anyway to finish an article she was writing for some magazine, so we decided to go home. I spent the next day writing a paper on the Italian Renaissance, which had been due before vacation started. I always left papers till the last minute, but once I got around to them, I'd whip them off in one day. I couldn't stand all the trouble of going to the library and finding all the right books only to have to do it again, so I worked like a fiend.

Chloe had called while I was out. Mom said she didn't leave any message, but said she would call back. She hadn't called by 9:30, so I dialed her number.

"Hello?"

I hesitated. "Hi—is this Julie?"

"Yeah. Hi, Val."

"Hi! Hey, I didn't know you were home! You weren't supposed to come till next week. When did you come?"

There was silence for a moment.

"Val, I don't know if you know this, but our father passed away last night."

My head reeled and I began to feel sick.

"What do you mean?" I said, my palm sweating on the receiver. Why didn't Chloe tell Mom when she called?

"He died in his sleep. He was taking a nap and his heart gave out."

"No. He couldn't have. I mean—Oh, Julie, I—"

"That's O.K.," she said, controlling her voice carefully.

Why do people say, "It's O.K."?

"Where's Chloe? Was she home?"

"No. She was with you. She's out with Mom now." I held the receiver tightly, unable to speak. "Hello?"

"I'm here—oh, Julie," I said again, choking. "When is—?"

"The wake is tomorrow."

Wake? Oh, God, I thought. An open coffin. At Jewish funerals the coffins are always closed. I took a deep breath.

"Where do I go?"

She gave me the address of the funeral parlor, and I hung up.

9

I PUT ON a dark skirt the next day and went to the funeral parlor. When I stepped out of the elevator, I saw people milling about, and standing in hushed little groups; it all looked like an underwater ballet. I stood awkwardly, not knowing what to do, and then Chloe came toward me. At first I didn't recognize her. She was wearing a pale silk blouse and black skirt; her otherwise pink cheeks were chalky and drawn, and her eyes were puffy. I was shocked; I'd never seen her like that. She looked so worn, I wanted to scoop her up and tell her everything was all right, but all I could do was stand there helplessly. I glanced over her shoulder, and seeing the open coffin and Mr. Fox's profile over at the back of the room, I gasped involuntarily.

"Val?" she whispered, and embraced me. I put my arms around her, feeling her thin shoulder blades beneath her blouse. I saw the coffin once more and shuddered, turning my head sideways so I wouldn't have to look as the tears began to come. Chloe took my shoulders and held me back.

"Don't cry," she said, brushing at my cheek. I should be comforting her, and here I am crying, I thought dismally. Her eyes were brimming and she took my hand.

"Do you want to see him? You don't have to." I nodded, and we walked over toward the coffin, stopping a few feet away.

"He looks like he always did," I said in a trance. "Like you could just wake him up." It's not so bad, seeing him like this, I thought. We stared at him for what seemed like ages, and then backed away.

"How come you didn't tell my mom when you called?"

"I didn't want her to feel sorry for me," Chloe said, looking at our feet. "I just wish I could have said goodbye. He was the best. . . ." She buried her head in my sweater and wept silently.

People kept trying to act as though nothing had happened; they asked Chloe and me about school and all, and Chloe was polite to all of them, but all I could think of was Mr. Fox lying there like that, only yards away from us. I wanted to pull Chloe away someplace where she could grieve, instead of pretending to be interested in the conversations people kept drumming up, but I couldn't. I stayed with her for hours. Before I left, I went over to say good-bye to Mrs. Fox.

"Oh, Valerie, are you leaving?" she said in a tired voice.

"Yes." I bit my lip for a moment and then kissed her quickly on the cheek. "I'll be back tomorrow."

"Thank you for coming."

I nodded, and Chloe walked me to the elevator.

I hardly spoke to Chloe the rest of the week after the funeral. I was afraid to call her house, and she only called me once and hardly said anything. After school started, it was the same; she even seemed to be avoiding me. Whenever I saw her she'd be walking down the halls wearily, as though she'd given up somehow. She didn't even try to hide if she was out of uniform when Olmsted was around. I went to a couple of dances alone and met a boy whose sister was in our class, and he was actually pretty interesting; I gave him my number and he'd called a few times. I tried telling Chloe about him, but she just stared at me, looking so dispirited I wanted to cry.

One night after Ben went to bed I was sitting in the kitchen with Mom. I'd been feeling sort of grumpy and depressed lately and began spending more time with her, just so I wouldn't have to be alone. I'd been wanting to ask somebody about my daydreams, and since Mr. Fox died I'd given up on telling Chloe, so I decided to poke around with asking Mom.

"Ma?"

"What?"

"If people think awful things, does that make them awful?" I said.

"Like what awful things?"

"Well, like—like wanting to murder people."

"I want to murder people all the time, but that doesn't make me awful," Mom said sensibly, lighting up a cigarette. "Everyone thinks things like that. That doesn't mean you're going to do it."

"Yeah, but—well," I said, thinking, How am I going to get an answer without telling her anything? "Well, how about perverts? Is everyone a potential pervert?"

Mom laughed. "What do you mean by perverted?"

That's the whole problem, I thought dismally. That's what I'm trying to find *out*.

"Well, like someone who fantasizes about sleeping with a dog, or something," I said, patting myself mentally for being prudent enough not to say "cat." Ben and I had been bugging Mom for ages to let us get a cat.

"Well, I'd say someone who thinks about that is pretty strange," she said. "But if all the person does is think, he's not a pervert. Or she. Pardon me. Whoever."

"What if the person did it?" I said miserably, knowing I wasn't getting anyplace.

"Then I guess some people would call it perverted," Mom said simply.

"Well then, how about gay people?" Ah, now I was getting down to it.

"I don't know," Mom said seriously. "I've been brought up to think it's wrong. But who am I to judge? I know a lot of happy homosexual couples."

"You *do*?" I said, amazed.

"Sure I do. Much better off than a lot of married people too, I can tell you. I always say, what people do in the privacy of their own home is their business."

"But is it *perverted*?" I insisted.

"I don't know."

"Oh," I said, and lost my nerve. I can't ask her. I can't ask her about heterosexual people who sometimes have homosexual fantasies. All she'd have to do is look at me and she'd know it was me. Besides, I don't think I've ever had a *sexual* fantasy, I told myself. I never thought about actually having sex with anyone. All I thought about was touching, and it's always been with guys, before this. Like Dr. Elgin, or Keith, the first guy who ever felt me up. Now that was fantastic, I thought, remembering. Is that a sexual fantasy? What about when I think about Chloe? How can someone have a sexual fantasy until they have sex and know what to think about? I mean, you have to do it before you know what you'd *like* to do, I said to myself logically. I hardly even have a frame of reference. Boy, aren't I intellectual! I came out of my daze, and Mom was staring at me.

"Thanks, Mom," I said, feeling embarrassed.

"For what?"

"Well, for not dissolving when I asked you all this stuff!"

"See?" she said triumphantly. "I'm getting better. When I was a little girl, people didn't talk of such things, and *never* to their mothers."

"Yeah, well, I bet gay couples didn't roam the streets of Europe either," I said. "Not like they do here."

"No. It wasn't the kind of thing you made public if you

could help it. I suppose it's better this way," she said, looking like a confused child. Well, don't look at me, I thought, feeling a little resentful. Here I am, this confused kid, trying to figure things out; why should I have to worry that *she's* worried because she's as confused as I am? Are there mothers who know the answers? Nah, I figured. There are just mothers who pretend they do. I just wish she wouldn't look so vulnerable. I decided to do what I'd been thinking of doing ever since that day on Crow Hill; I'd go ask the biology teacher at school. I didn't have to take biology till eleventh grade, but I knew Miss Udry from the cross-town bus. It was her first year at Garfield too, and we'd gotten pretty friendly. When I first met her I thought she was a senior or something, she looked so young. This was her first job. Also, she lived on the West Side and she was Jewish, and I felt a certain kinship when we boarded the bus together. Yeah, I thought. I'll go to her classroom during prayers tomorrow; maybe she'll be there.

"Val? Yoo hoo!" Mom was waving her hand in front of my face. "Come in, Valerie." I smiled. "How's Chloe?"

"Oh, O.K., I guess," I lied. I didn't want to talk to Mom about Chloe.

"Is she doing O.K.? Poor thing," Mom said sadly, shaking her head. I felt annoyed at her for bringing it up. I'm not being fair, wanting to turn her on and off like that. I ask her all kinds of questions and she's patient and understanding, and then she asks me about Chloe and I'm thinking, Shut up. I don't feel like talking about her. What's the matter with me, anyway?

"Why don't you invite her over? She hasn't been here

in ages," Mom was saying. Ha, I thought. Like I haven't tried. Every time I asked Chloe to come over she said she couldn't, she had to stay home with her mother so she wouldn't have to be alone in the house, or that she had to go to her father's office to help straighten out his things.

"She's been busy keeping her mother company," I said brusquely, and went off to my room.

Later on that night I dialed Chloe's number. I kept calling her as I always had, even though she didn't call me that much; the problem was she didn't talk much any more, so I wound up gabbing till I was sick of listening to myself just to fill the silence.

"Hi, it's me. Old faithful," I said.

"Oh, hi."

"Whatcha doing?"

"Nothing." There was a long pause. "Cutting up the new *Vogue*, actually."

"You sound enthused." I heard faint music and voices. "What's that?"

"What? Oh, my mother's just yelling."

"Why?" I heard Mrs. Fox in the background, yelling, ". . . crazy nut, what does he think he's doing, waking up the neighbors, somebody's going to report . . . ."

"Hey, Chloe! What's going on?"

She giggled weakly. "There's this guy about three houses down from us who plays the bagpipe. He goes into his backyard every night to play. You can hear it all over."

"Wow!" I said, intrigued. "What kind of person is he?"

"Oh, old. Well, not old. Sort of oldish. He has a beard and wears those old-fashioned baggy slacks. I've seen him a few times getting his mail. He's neat-looking—even sexy, in a way."

"And he plays the bagpipe? In his backyard? At night? I love it!"

"Yeah, me too," Chloe said, sounding a little better. "But it's driving my mother up a wall. You should hear her carry on about it. It's really funny." I heard strains of music through the receiver. "It's really beautiful, you know? When the moon is out I can see him out my window."

"Oh, Chloe, that sounds so positively enchanting," I said dreamily.

"I know. I sit by the window whenever he's out there and listen. It makes me feel—"

"Like some mystical mysterious girl everyone wonders about?" I suggested.

She laughed. "Yeah. And then I hear my mother screeching, 'That maniac, he must be *crazy* playing that thing in the middle of the night! I ought to report it!' And there goes the mystery!"

"Chloe, listen. Can you come over and see me?" I said timidly.

"Well—I don't have time right now," she hedged.

"Chloe, come on. I never get to see you anymore! Sleep over this weekend."

"I can't."

"Why not?"

"I can't leave my mother alone. She gets depressed and she hates being in the house alone."

I was getting angry. "Chloe, damn it, I know it's rough

for your mother, but you've got to live too! You've got to get out of there too, it's not good for you, it isn't *fair*—"

"Val!" she said loudly, choking a sob. "Don't you understand anything? I don't *want* to leave her alone!" Suddenly I heard the receiver clunk down. She'd hung up on me. Dumbfounded, I put down the phone.

The next morning I went up to the biology lab. I got there really early, and sat like a zombie on one of the desks staring at the large skeleton model standing in the corner. One of the hands had fallen off and been tied back on. Chloe and I had wanted to nab it to add to a morbid 3-D collage we'd been constructing at my house, but we'd never gotten around to it. It dangled precariously and I fixed my eyes on it, lost to the world, till the door opened. Miss Udry flipped on the light and jumped when she saw me.

"Hi!" she said, surprised.

"Hi."

"What are you doing in here now? You should be at prayers."

I grimaced. "I wanted to talk to you."

"Me?" She smiled agreeably. "Sure. Just let me get undone here," she said, taking off her sweater and rearranging a stack of papers on her desk. She came and sat down on a desk across from me.

"You certainly don't fit in here," I remarked. "You're nothing like the other teachers. That's a compliment, by the way."

"Oh, come on. They're not so bad once you get to know them. Just a little uptight."

"A little!" I laughed. I caught a whiff of her perfume. I know that smell, I thought. From where? I inhaled deeply.

"Oh! You smell just like the hospital," I exclaimed. She looked taken aback. "I mean one of the nurses," I explained quickly. "She wore that perfume."

"When were you in the hospital?"

"I wasn't. My grandmother was, last fall. She died of cancer."

"Your grandmother died of cancer last fall? Gee, I didn't know that. You never mentioned it."

"No," I said, thinking back. It seemed so long ago. That whole time she was sick and after she died had become one long rainy interlude in my memory; little things like smelling someone's perfume or seeing someone who wore her hair in a bun reminded me sharply of Grandma, and then it would fade again.

"I'm sorry," Miss Udry said.

"Yeah. So am I." I looked at my knees. How do I start this conversation?

"What's on your mind?"

"I was wondering about gay people," I said quickly. "Actually, I was wondering about regular—I mean, heterosexual people who think about things gay people do. Like a heterosexual guy thinking about another guy that way," I said. What a muddle.

"Oh, you mean heterosexuals who have homosexual fantasies?"

That was easy enough! I thought, a little relieved. Does she know why I'm asking? She must.

"Yeah," I continued. "I mean—is it sick?"

"Not at all. It's normal, as a matter of fact."

"It is?"

"Sure. A lot of people probably do become sexually attracted to someone of their own sex at one time or another."

Sexually *attracted*—so that's what my daydreams mean, I thought.

"They do?" I said. "Then how come most people think gay people are sick?"

"Because it scares them," she said simply.

"But then, are heterosexuals the way they are just because they're trained to be by society?"

"Boy, that's a heavy for eight-thirty in the morning! I can't answer that. I don't know."

"Well," I ventured. "Do you think it's 'unnatural' to have fantasies like that?"

She looked at me quizzically. I held my breath waiting for her to admit she knew why I was asking. She paused for a moment, and then said, "I don't know, Val. I guess you can't judge people by their fantasies. People think all sorts of things."

"Do you think people who are gay are unnatural?"

"Well, I do—no, I suppose they're not—I don't know, you know that? I really don't know what to tell you."

I sighed. "That's O.K. Nobody else does either." Someone peeped in the door, and Miss Udry motioned for them to wait outside. "Oh, it's O.K. I've got to go anyway."

"Sure. Listen, come talk to me again, O.K.?" She put

her hand on my shoulder. "Are you O.K.? You look a little green."

"Oh, I always look a little green. It's the uniform reflecting off my face."

Miss Udry laughed. "O.K. Thanks for coming to see me."

I beamed back at her. "Thanks for saying thanks." Boy, and she never came out and asked why I wanted to know all this. By some silent agreement, we had discussed it without acknowledging it. Still, I thought, I don't know any more than I did before. It was just like with Mom—talking theories was easy. But in the end, neither one of them had an answer.

I had study hall third period and went out to Carl Schurz Park. It was kind of a gray day and there weren't too many people there, just a few people pushing baby carriages and strollers. This one little boy with strawberry-colored curls and big green eyes waved at me, and I smiled in spite of myself and waved back. It makes me feel so good when little kids wave at me; like they can tell I like them or something, which I do. Then I went to my usual spot on the promenade. There was a little boat with a dirty yellow sign saying SUNOCO going by, and I leaned on the railing to watch. I haven't felt this lonely since the beginning of the year, I thought. I missed Chloe. Things weren't as much fun without her. Even just running around school, cutting prayers, going to Third Avenue, didn't have the allure she gave it. I should think she'd need me more than ever; I could sure use a nice loyal friend like me, I thought grumpily. I wonder how I'd act if my dad died. Would I lean on a friend? Maybe I'd run home and keep Mom company, like Chloe's doing. Maybe you just want to be around your family when someone dies; come to think of it, I ran home right after school every day when Grandma died, even though it was depressing being there. Of course, I didn't know Chloe then; but maybe I'd have done it anyway. Suddenly I felt a hand on my neck. I froze, and Chloe poked her head around over my shoulder, giving a ferocious, toothy smile.

"Hiya, dollface. Thought I'd find you here." My heart leaped, but I said nothing. "I'm sorry about last night."

"That's O.K."

"I was upset."

I looked closely at her face. Her eyes had dark circles under them, and she looked exhausted. "I know. You look like hell."

She nodded.

"Chloe, listen, I didn't mean to make you mad. I was only thinking of what would be best for *you*, you know?"

"I know."

"I mean, I worry about you. You look so defeated all the time, and you never want to do anything or even just visit, and—" I stopped short, afraid I was going to cry.

"Oh, Val," she said tenderly.

"And I miss you, that's all. I know that sounds selfish. I wish I could make you feel better, but I know I can't."

"But you do make me feel better, just by being there," she said, and looked down the promenade. "Val, what's at the end of this?"

"I think a pier or something. Let's go see."

We began walking along the river together in silence. Suddenly Patty came onto the promenade from a small path up ahead and began walking in our direction. Chloe curled her lip in disgust.

"Hi, Val, hi, Chloe," she said as she walked by, staring at us with an odd expression on her face.

"Boy," Chloe said when Patty was beyond hearing distance, "ever since my father died everyone looks at me like I've got leukemia or something! You should see Olmsted, patting my head in the halls . . . I could just puke!"

"Chloe, they're just trying to be nice," I said.

"Oh, yeah? Well I don't need their being nice. They act like they're scared to death of me! You know how everyone's always after us for being out of uniform and being late—well, now nobody says *anything*. I could come to school wearing purple feathers and they wouldn't say a word, but before he died they'd have crucified me. Who needs their phony-baloney sympathy? I hate being felt sorry for."

We walked on in silence. Would I want people to feel sorry for me if my father died? I thought. When I broke my leg in sixth grade, everyone made a big deal out of it and I relished every minute; I even kept using crutches three days after they took the cast off and pretended my leg was too weak to walk on. But I guess it's different when your father dies.

"Listen, Val, when vacation starts, would you come sleep over at my house?"

My face lit up. "Sure. Sure I would!"

"See, I don't want to leave my mother alone, but I don't want to invite anyone over yet, you know? It'd just be depressing anyway."

"Yeah," I said. "Well, I'll probably be away in June. I guess I didn't tell you. I'm getting a mother's-helper job."

"Yeah? How?"

"Friends of the funeral-parlor people. The pay'll probably be lousy, but I could use the money and maybe I'll get to go someplace glamourous. So I'd have to come as soon as school is over," I said, wanting to pin her down. "Chloe, you're my best and only friend. You're the greatest. You won't get rid of *me* easily!"

She laughed, for the first time in ages, it seemed. "O.K. The *second* we get out of this godforsaken place."

"Promise?"

"Absolutely-positively-no-doubt-about-it—is that how it goes?"

Should I tell her about Miss Udry? I wondered. But then I'd be assuming she felt that way about me, too, and if I was wrong she might be scared to death of me. Christ, she has enough on her mind, I thought, feeling guilty. I won't say anything. I smiled at her, and she grabbed my arm and we began running toward the pier.

10

SO THE weeks went by and spring seemed to be over before it began. I went out once with Ian, the guy I met at the dance, to Central Park; if you want my advice, don't sit in the grass there. I nearly sat in dog shit twice; I'd have died if I had! Ian didn't talk very much the whole afternoon, but whenever I met a guy who didn't say much, I told myself he was deep and it was up to me to rouse his sensitive soul. Usually there wasn't anything to rouse, but I liked Ian anyway; I don't have to *marry* him, I thought. He kissed me twice and tried sticking his tongue in my mouth, but it felt like a raw hotdog and I made him stop. I was glad he tried, though. I was a little nervous the whole time we were together and scared I'd say the wrong thing, but all in all it was a pleasant afternoon and we agreed to meet up in the Hamptons, which was where my job was going to be.

I was lonely, though; without Chloe, even going out with Ian seemed drab. It wasn't the same telling Mom about things like that. I guess it sounds weird saying, "without Chloe," because we saw each other every day. But between her running down to her father's law firm after school and her not really listening or talking to me when I called her, I *felt* like she was gone. It's hard to explain. It's like I had a hole inside, and I kept waiting for her to come back so it would go away.

Then suddenly, bang, school was over. I couldn't believe how quickly the time had gone by. I did well on all my exams, even French, but I think Marese was just being nice. She had developed a real soft spot for Chloe and me, her front-row pupils. People began bringing home their gym stuff, and Chloe forgot her locker combination. We had to get the janitor to break the lock, and then it took her three days to cart home all the junk she had accumulated. I told her she should take the things she wanted all at once and throw the rest out, so no one would steal anything, but she couldn't part with any of it and pointed out that no one in their right mind would go through her locker looking for something to steal. When she said that, I had to agree. Finally we all cleaned out our cubbies, throwing out pages and pages of last-minute-panic notes we swallowed whole before exams and forgot the instant they were finished, and we hauled home piles of textbooks we'd probably stuff in some closet and forget about. I can't throw out a book, even a math book. The posters some kids had put on the homeroom walls came down, leaving nothing but yellow tape marks, and the room seemed hollow and unfamiliar, as though it had forgotten us. I knew it would be strange to see someone from the class behind mine sitting at *my* desk in the fall.

Chloe asked me to sleep over after graduation. Graduation wasn't any big thing for us, since we didn't know any of the seniors. We had to march in uniform, sing two songs, and that was it. I felt a little sentimental when the whole school sang "Jerusalem," but I was glad the year was over and I wasn't a "new girl" anymore; in the fall I'll be an *old* girl, I thought. I guess it's not till you've been at a school for a whole year and can show a new girl where some classroom is that she can't find that you feel like you belong.

It was early evening and pleasantly cool when we all piled out of the school building for the last time, and Mrs. Fox was waiting in the car to drive us home. She told us she was going out for the evening to her brother's house, and Chloe pounded my knee happily with her fist.

After we all had dinner and Mrs. Fox left, Chloe and I made some popcorn and sat down in the den to watch "Carousel." It was a sad movie, and I was depressed enough as it was; Chloe kept staring at her father's chair in the corner of the room, sitting there expectantly in a half-reclined position. It seemed to me I'd never seen an emptier chair.

"How's your beautiful-lady collection?" I said after a while, turning down the TV.

"Oh, nearly finished. I'm going to start on the collage after a few more cutting sessions."

"That's great. We should take each other's pictures, then."

"Oh, that reminds me—I wanted to show you a book I got." She jumped up and ran out of the den, reappearing a moment later. "Photographs of France. Rodney gave it to me. It cost a mint." She smiled, and sat down next to me on the couch. We looked at each picture for a long time, talking and pointing things out.

"Oh, Paris," I sighed, looking at a street scene. "I'd love to go to Paris. And Rome. With you, of course," I added. "You know, my grandmother wanted to be an artist."

"Yeah?" Chloe said, looking interested.

"Yeah. Her father promised to send her to art school in Paris. Then he died, and she never went."

"But that's so *tragic*!" she exclaimed.

"I know. Maybe I'll go instead. It'll be my mission." I sat back thoughtfully. "I really loved her, you know? I don't think she knew how much I loved her. You know how some older people look like they've given up?" Chloe nodded. "She never did. Not ever. I never told her any of this stuff," I said wistfully.

"That's O.K., Val," Chloe said, touching my hand.

"No. It isn't O.K. You should—you should tell people things. I've been thinking about it a lot. People should be kind to each other, you know?" I gazed off hazily and focused on a spot on the wall. It kind of disturbed me that I'd been thinking about death so much. It hadn't seemed real when Grandma died, but it became real as soon as I started thinking of things I wanted to tell her and then remembered I couldn't. And then when Mr. Fox died, I realized Mom and Dad were going to die too, something I never really believed before that. I bet Mom never thought her mother would die when she was my age, I thought. It really scared me, and I began thinking twice about things. Like if Dad wanted to talk to me and I didn't have time I'd make time, thinking: Someday he'll die and I'll wish I could spend more time with him— only now I can choose, and then I won't be able to. People might think I was sick to think that way, but I don't think it's morbid or anything. There's nothing morbid about death, it's just a fact and people wish it wasn't. So they don't think about it in time. It isn't even bad that if someone's dying you're nicer to them; it's just that knowing it's going to happen makes you more thoughtful. People are so dumb sometimes. Someone dies and they think of all the things they put off or never said and wish they had, and you'd think it would change them. But they just keep wishing the dead person were back so they could do things right, instead of paying attention to the people that aren't dead yet.

"Val?" Chloe said awkwardly, bringing me back to earth. "I think you're beautiful."

"Oh, bunk. You don't have to say that."

"I don't *have* to say *anything*."

I smiled. I should tell her about my daydreams, I thought for the hundredth time. She won't mind; I don't *think* she will.

"Oh, I'm so depressed," she moaned. "Hey, there's some white wine in the fridge. Want some?"

"Sure, why not?"

She went and filled two jelly glasses and brought them in, handing me one of them. "This is good," I said, after tasting it, and took a large sip. "It makes me feel warm all over." We sprawled out on the rug with our jelly glasses, the television forgotten.

"Val, did I tell you about that lawyer? Remember, the one who used to make passes at me all the time when I went to see my father?"

"No, tell me."

"Well, one night last week I was up there, and my mother had to leave early, so he offered to drive me home. He lives in Riverdale too and I really didn't feel like taking the bus, so I said O.K."

"And?"

"He started complaining about his wife, and how she doesn't understand him, and how miserable he is."

"He's married?"

"*Yes*. He went on and on."

"That's terrible."

"He pulled over to the side of the road," she went on. "He wanted to know if he could see me, and I didn't know what to do! Here I was in this car with this married man who used to work with my *father*, and he was practically asking me to have an affair with him! Me!"

"Oh, Chloe, what did you do?"

"I said no, I don't think so. I didn't want to hurt his feelings." I gave her an exasperated look. "You know, Val, when your father dies, everything's so different. I feel so old." I listened to her, transfixed. "I was always Daddy's little girl, you know? I mean, Julie was the oldest, but I was his little princess. That's what he called me. It was so weird, being in that car. I'm not his little girl anymore." She paused, finishing her wine and placing the glass on the table. "He was always so glad to see me when I came home, even just from your house. Now I can't stand coming home."

I held her hand. What can I tell her? I thought. That it scares me to hear her say that, because I know it will happen to me too? That I wish I could help her? How can I help anyone?

"How's your mother doing?"

"Oh, rotten," Chloe said with a groan. "It's terrible to see her, Val. She's so depressed all the time. I keep her company every night, but there's nothing to talk about. I can't tell her things like you can tell your mother."

"I'm lucky, I guess."

"You sure are. And what's my mother got to look forward to? Getting old. She'll never remarry, and after I leave home she'll be all alone. She doesn't even have friends. Not close friends."

"Why not?" I said, feeling pleasantly woozy.

"I guess because she has such high standards, people

disappoint her, and she's hard to get close to anyway. So she doesn't make friends. You know, in a crazy way I feel like I should become her companion and live with her after we get out of school."

I looked at her in horror. "Chloe, you can't do that!"

"Oh, I know, and I wouldn't. I'd go crazy. But—do you know what I mean?"

I nodded. Poor Chloe: first she feels responsible for her father, and now she feels responsible for her mother.

"Chloe, you're too young to worry about stuff like that," I said.

"Oh?" She glanced up at me and I touched her cheek.

"Chloe, you're my best friend. My only one. I'd do anything to make you feel better. Anything, just name it. That doesn't help much, does it?"

"Yes, it does." She got up rather unsteadily to turn off the TV, laughing at herself. "I think we drank that wine too fast, I feel really drowsy."

"Me too. In a nice way, though."

"Mm. Let's go upstairs, O.K.? I don't want to be down here swaying when my mother gets home."

"Sure. Are we sleeping up there?"

"Yup."

We climbed the stairs and walked through the bedroom to Chloe's painting room.

"Your own studio," I said dreamily.

Chloe laughed. "My mother says it's a dump," she said, mimicking her mother's voice.

"I love dumps." The room looked the way it always did; easels, oil paints, cartons overflowing with clothing everywhere. Chloe dug up a few pairs of old shorts and tossed them to me.

"Want 'em?"

"Yeah, thanks. Chlo, where'll you be all summer?"

"Oh, we might go away for a couple of weeks this month, to Connecticut. Then I'll just be here. Maybe work at my mom's law firm."

"Good. I'll probably be in and out of the city after this stupid job."

We wandered back into the bedroom.

"You sleep in here," Chloe said.

"What about you?"

"I can sleep on the cot in there."

"But it's stuffy in there! I'll sleep in there." But she wouldn't let me. We changed into big shirts and I got into bed and so did she. Five minutes later I heard her voice in the dark.

"Val? Are you asleep?"

"Are you crazy?"

"It's hot in here. Do you mind if I sleep with you?"

"Come on."

She stepped in like a ghost, her shirttail bobbing, the moonlight giving her an unearthly glow. "Get in!" I said, and she did.

"Thanks a lot. It's much cooler in here."

I can't believe it, I thought. I'm actually insulted because she only came in to be cooler. Didn't she? Sure she did. She doesn't think of twisted things like I do! Or are they twisted? I want to tell her, I thought. When it's dark and she can't see my face. I lay there working up the courage to do it, and finally said, "Chloe?" but she'd fallen asleep. A little relieved, I looked around at the vague outlines of furniture, feeling comfortably hazy and liquid from the wine. Chloe's clothing on top of the dresser looked like an elephant looming in the dark, the way it was piled. Maybe I am horrible after all, I thought. Maybe she'd never think of me except as a friend. But then maybe she would. But why hasn't she said anything? She'd be scared, like I am, probably. But Chloe isn't scared of things like that; she never listens to what anyone says and she doesn't care what people think. No, that's not true; she cares what her mother thinks. Oh, rats. What's wrong with me?

Suddenly Chloe trembled and began to whimper.

"Chloe, what's wrong?" I said, propping myself up on my elbow and reaching out to her with my other hand. "Chloe, wake up."

She slowly turned her head around and blinked. "She was yelling at me and I was yelling back, it was my fault he died—"

I reached for her shoulder impulsively and my hand met her body.

"Shh, Chloe, it's O.K., it's only a dream," I whispered. Where am I touching her? I wondered. I shifted my hand, trying to find her head, but it wasn't there. Then it hit me. I, Valerie Hoffman, am touching her breast. But why hadn't she moved away or turned around? My heart pounding, I went on, slipping my other arm around her and stroking her back gently, the way Mom used to stroke mine when I cried.

"But it was my fault," she said, crying softly.

"No, it wasn't. You weren't even there. It was just a bad dream. Shh, come on."

"Oh, Val," she said, and placed her hand over mine, the one that was on her breast. She held it there for a while, and then I eased it around her back and massaged her, holding her close to me. This isn't sick at all, I thought, closing my eyes. Everything I'm doing I'm doing because it's what my instinct says to do. She felt warm and frail beneath her shirt as she huddled closer to me. My entire body felt as though a generator had gone on. Miss Udry's words came back to me: sexual attraction. Is that what I'm feeling right now—me, normal Valerie —from Riverside Drive? She *wants* me to do this, I thought. I'm not making it up; it's happening. But what is it that's happening? Only that we're holding each other and it feels good. Is it wrong to feel good about doing this?

Chloe lowered her head and rested it on my breasts. They must make a great pillow, I thought, laughing silently at myself. Maybe they're not so bad to have after all. My arm was still around her, and I kept it there. She gave a little sigh and seemed to fall asleep.

Then I heard footsteps. A bolt of fear shot through me: Mrs. Fox must be home. Is she coming up the stairs? I wanted to get up and shut the door, but before I had a chance to move, I saw the top of her head above the banister outside the room. I closed my eyes and froze, waiting.

The footsteps stopped. I lifted my lids just enough to see what was going on. Mrs. Fox was standing at the top of the stairs, peering in at us. I closed my eyes again and held my breath; it was the longest minute of my life. When I heard footsteps again I opened my eyes to look. She was gone.

What did she see? I thought wildly. What did she think? Chloe lay still as a rock and after a while bent her leg up and rested it on mine, moving her head up onto her pillow. I watched her sleeping face, my mind blank with fear; I don't know when I finally fell asleep.

Dim yellow-gray light pushed its way into my thick sleep. I squinted and opened my eyes with difficulty, as the events of the night slowly surfaced in my mind, waking me with a sickening lurch. Did I dream it? No, not this time. I rubbed the sleep out of my eyes and looked at my watch. 6:45. Pretty soon they'll wake up, I thought; pretty soon we'll have to have breakfast together. Is Mrs. Fox going to say anything? Should I tell Chloe she saw us? Is Chloe going to pretend last night never happened? How could she, even if she wanted to? But what does it mean? I looked over at her face poking out of the sheets, her hair spread over the pillow. I'm scared, I thought. I feel like I was caught at something terrible. The light coming through the window was cold and unsympathetic.

I crept out of bed and put on my rumpled clothes, which I'd left in a heap on the floor. Fully dressed and holding my shoes, I looked back at Chloe's sleeping figure once more and then inched my way stealthily down the stairs. I got my bag from the den, opened the back door as quietly as I could, and ran down the gravel driveway and up to the bus stop at the end of the street, shivering in the morning sun.

11

I WAITED three days for Chloe to call.
Every time the phone rang, my heart skipped a beat, but
it was never her; whenever I came home from doing an
errand or buying things I needed for Easthampton, like
Tampax and deodorant and stuff, I asked Mom if anyone
had called, but no one had. I started to call her twice,
but hung up both times before I got to the last number.
I really drove myself crazy trying to figure out why Chloe
hadn't called. Mrs. Fox must have told her she saw;
maybe she even forbade Chloe to have anything to do
with me, I thought, forgetting that no one could stop

Chloe from doing anything if she really wanted to. Otherwise, why wouldn't she call me? It was either that, or else I was wrong thinking Chloe had wanted me to touch her. Maybe it was just the wine, and when she remembered everything the next day she was disgusted. She's probably scared of me; maybe she thinks I'm horrible and never even wants to see me again.

So I brooded for three days, knowing that finally something had happened that we couldn't ignore. When we see each other again, I thought, how can we go on being friends as though nothing had happened? It isn't something vague we can avoid talking about, the way it was before the other night, I told myself. What will she say? What will I say? Why won't she *call* me?

Then, before I could even get up the courage to call Chloe and say good-bye, I was whisked off to the Hamptons.

The job was a disaster from the start. The Baskwells turned out to be the type of rich people that tried to look poor and had scads of friends as sham as they were, and they all went to dumb parties and drank and talked about dumb things and laughed at jokes that weren't funny and the men made passes at their friends' wives. I knew that because a few of the parties were at our house, and since it was too noisy to read or think, I listened through the paper-thin walls of my room. You could hear everything perfectly because the walls were made of cheap beaverboard; the outside was plain and gray, like all the other beach houses.

The Baskwells were just renting the place, so I couldn't blame them for the decor, which consisted of things like a big fake fish hanging over a big fake fireplace in the living room, and furniture sets that looked like they'd been won on a TV game show. I heard them saying it was tacky to some friends of theirs, but I didn't think much of their style either. They were the type of people that would poke holes in their jeans. The first three nights I couldn't take a bath because Mrs. Baskwell, who was tall, flat-chested, frosted blond and had mean green eyes and high cheekbones, had filled the tub with bleach and blue jeans. I guess it was part of their looking "rugged." Mr. and Mrs. Baskwell were always talking about being "rugged" and looking "rugged," only they couldn't pronounce their r's, so it was "wugged." I laughed to myself whenever they said it, thinking what a kick Chloe would get out of it, and then remembered I'd decided not to write to her. I tried writing a few times the first week, but the letters never sounded right. I was afraid of not being able to see her reaction to what I was trying to say, or even worse, of the possibility that she wouldn't read them. So I tore them up. If I tell her anything, I decided, it has to be in person.

It's funny, you'd think being in a house in Easthampton right by the beach would be nice, but it was hell. If Mr. and Mrs. Baskwell rubbed me the wrong way, it was nothing compared to their three kids. They drove me bananas. Colin was seven, and the eldest. He was hyperactive, and his hands never stopped flailing and thrashing. If he wasn't hitting Lilli, who was two, he was punching Stevie, and then *he* got wild; and if he wasn't doing that, he was hitting me, screaming and yelling the whole time. I was ready to quit and run out the door at least ten times each day, and ordinarily I'm not a quitter, but I was really miserable and those damn kids threw tantrums like they were going out of style. According to Mrs. Baskwell, however, I was not to reprimand them. I was to be calm and ignore it. She had this nasty way of saying things, like I was some sort of monster for wanting to discipline her kids, so I didn't argue; I gritted my teeth a lot.

"*Mommy*, I'm too *tired* [scream] to brush my teeth—*you* do it." Colin shrieked like that every night, and half the time Lilli would wake up and start howling, and when that happened I wanted to kill them both. Stevie was no prize, either; he threw rocks at other people's cars. Really, that's what he'd do when we weren't at the beach, just sit in the driveway throwing rocks at cars. Mrs. Baskwell acted like she'd never heard of discipline; I think she must have read some screwy permissive child-care book. After a week of being there I found out she had an ulcer and took Librium (I checked the cabinet in her bathroom) but I didn't feel sorry for her.

The second week it rained almost every day; you can imagine what being cooped up in that house was like. It was a nightmare. In between whining, "Whadda we do *now*," Colin broke three vases in the living room and Lilli got hold of Mr. Baskwell's razor and cut her lip. Of course, that was my fault; I was too busy scraping off the Silly Putty Stevie got on the couch to watch her. It was like that for days. My hair frizzed out like blown circuits, I caught a cold, and life was never less appealing.

The first decent afternoon after the rain, Mrs. Baskwell made me take the kids into the ocean, which wasn't unreasonable except that I was sick, and they deducted $1.50 for a bottle of Dristan from my $45.00 for that week. By then Mrs. Baskwell had railroaded me into "helping out" with the housework too, which wasn't supposed to be part of the deal, and "helping out" meant doing everything. I don't know why I didn't tell her to go jump in the ocean; that's what Chloe would do, I thought to myself one morning as I was changing the linen. Chloe would tell her off; she wouldn't take this crap. Chloe! I sighed, feeling miserable, and finished pulling off Colin's top-bunk sheets.

I met Anne on the beach one day. Maryanna Porco, to be exact. She was a mother's helper too, and she began visiting me in the evenings. She was kind of boring, Catholic like Chloe was (only I don't think Chloe believed a word of it), had the worst case of acne I'd ever seen, and she was very nice in a prim sort of way. She was a poor substitute for Chloe, but then anyone was, and I was grateful for her company.

"Colin wets his bed *every night!*" I told her one evening as we were whispering in my tiny room.

"Oh, boy," she said, rolling her eyes.

"And he won't let his parents close their bedroom door at night."

"Won't *let* them?"

"*She* lets that maniac *dictate* around here," I grumbled.

"You mean they sleep with the door open every night because of him?" I nodded. Once at two in the morning after they'd been out I opened my door a crack, listening for sounds coming from their bedroom: I thought maybe I'd hear them doing it, but they must have gone to sleep instead.

"And he sleepwalks, too," I continued. "He stumbles around and wails for his glasses. It spooks me out. I can't stand it here."

"You should quit. I can't believe they treat you the way they do."

"Believe it, believe it! I'm telling you, I'm housekeeper, baby-sitter, everything! Those damn kids wake up at five-thirty and I have to get up too."

"What?" Anne said, shocked.

"When do you get up?"

"Never till nine or nine-thirty. Sometimes Mrs. Farber makes Teddy his breakfast so I can sleep." This was unbelievable. "Hey, did you do that?" she said, pointing at a watercolor I'd done, which was on top of the dresser.

"Yeah, it's not very good," I said. "I have a friend who can paint really well."

"I think it's great," she said, getting up to examine it.

"Do you have a lot of friends?" I said suddenly.

"Well, I have three or four *close* friends," Anne said thoughtfully. "We always do things together. Do you?"

"No, just one."

She looked at me questioningly.

"I guess it depends on what you call a friend. I mean, I have people I talk to, but I only have one friend." I hope I do, I thought, a lump coming up in my throat.

"Why don't we go for a walk?" Anne suggested a moment later. It sounded like a good idea, and I went and and told the Baskwells we were going out for a while.

I began going for walks on the beach at night after that first time, usually alone. I sat sometimes and listened to the ocean, just listened, and looked at the stars. The sand was cold and clammy at night, but I didn't mind. I played my recorder sometimes, thinking of Chloe and the bagpipe man, and it sounded strange and magical in the thick, salty night air.

On my second day off, I met Ian in Easthampton. He was even better looking than I remembered him, and had as little to say as he had that day in Central Park, but I was so glad to get away from that house I didn't care. We went to the A & P and bought salami and rolls and beer, which I hate, and a whole bunch of other stuff, and had a picnic in a cemetery nearby. I had to do a lot of convincing to get him to agree to it; I told him about the time Chloe and I had gone down to Trinity Church, and he said he couldn't understand why we'd want to sit around in a cemetery in the snow.

We had our picnic under a tree, and afterward he started kissing me. We were at it for a long time, and then he tried getting my pants off. I noticed two people visiting a nearby gravestone who seemed to be looking in our direction, and I pushed him away. I wouldn't have let him do it anyway; feeling me up was one thing, but I wanted to be in love with someone before I let them do the rest. Maybe that's old-fashioned, but I couldn't feel good about it any other way.

In the late afternoon, Ian hitched back to Southampton and I walked back through Easthampton, past the white picket fences and big white houses with deep, cool, lush trees lining the street, and big bushes of blue hortensias in the yards. I finally got a ride back to Amagansett, and suddenly I knew I was going to be sick. Instead of going back to the Baskwells', I went to the Farbers' house, where Anne lived, and knocked on the door. Mrs. Farber answered, and I said, "Can I please throw up in your bathroom?"

I must have looked really green, because Mrs. Farber wordlessly took my bag and ushered me into the bathroom. Afterward, I fell asleep on Anne's bed, resolving never to eat salami again, and when I woke up I felt much better. We all sat in the living room and talked.

Anne, as I said, was nice and kind of quiet. But Mrs. Farber was great, and she hated the Baskwells. She was as sarcastic, cynical and bitchy as I was, and we had a blast.

"I can tell them and their friends a mile away," she said.

"Oh, yes, because they're all in their identical wugged-beachy-casual-outfits—"

"*Carefully* casual, of course."

"Of *course*. And they don't wear things because they like them, they wear them because they're 'in.' "

"Even if it looks terrible!" Mrs. Farber said, laughing. "The men's trunks are too small, and the women—"

"They all wear those disgusting skin-tight terry things," she said. "And they all sit on the beach and discuss their tennis clubs and plastic surgery and compare anklets. Very chic."

"Mm-hm." We knocked the kids, we knocked the Baskwells, we knocked everything.

"I'm going to quit," I told them gravely.

"When?"

"I told my father I was going to tell them some story about a sick relative, and he just said to tell him when to get me." I had told Mom and Dad about the Baskwells; when I told Mom about the Dristan, she let me talk to Dad while she went to pour herself some vodka. Mom absolutely never drinks. I couldn't even bring myself to tell her then that, not only was I a zookeeper for three satanic peewees, I was a housekeeper too; I finally told Dad when I was getting desperate to cut out.

"Why don't you tell them the truth? Those kids need three mothers' helpers!" Mrs. Farber was saying.

"I'm scared."

She rolled her eyes.

I called Dad the next day to confirm my plans; he would come on Saturday to get me. I told the Baskwells my story and they seemed to believe me, which was pretty amazing since it was the most transparent-sounding excuse I'd ever given. They were a little upset, because of the inconvenience, and began hunting immediately for a replacement for the remaining week and a half. As soon as I told them I was leaving, I began feeling better; for a while I'd toyed with the idea of getting Stevie run over by a truck or suffocating Lilli, but I didn't care anymore. I didn't have long to go.

On Thursday night, I went out to the beach. A bunch of boys were having a beer-drinking contest near where I usually sat, so I began walking. After a while I took off my sneakers and tied them together, carrying them over my shoulder. I walked a long way; it must have been close to midnight when I stopped at a little spot in between two dunes. There was a lot of wood lying around, pieces of broken fences and driftwood, and I threw down my sneakers and began making a small pile. Then I searched around and found several large rocks and placed them in a circle, digging a little pit inside and putting all the wood I'd collected into it. I found a book of matches in my back pocket and after fifteen minutes I had a fire. It was small at first, and crackled like a bowl of Rice Krispies in the wind. Then the flames began to shoot up, and I lay on the sand staring into it, thinking. Chloe, Chloe, Chloe—do you hate me? Am I terrible? You looked so innocent lying there in the morning . . . did I corrupt you? No, I thought, and then: if I had it to do all over again, I would do it the same way. Will you still run away and be a gypsy with me? I'm a captive princess, I thought, my eyes fixed on the licking tiger flames. And so are you. I see you dancing in the firelight on the empty beach; it's where you belong. Did I do something wrong? Why didn't you call me? Do you feel guilty too? Or just scared of me? You're never afraid. How can I face Garfield without you?

After I don't know how long, I got up and took off my clothes. It's now or never, I thought, taking a deep breath. I ran naked into the black, roaring sea and looked down at my body, bobbing like so many globes. I'd never gone swimming at night and had always wanted to try it. Soon I was running back to the fire, which was slowly going out, and shook myself quickly before I began getting dressed. My arms and legs were covered with goosebumps. I looked down at my breasts in the light that was left and thought, they're not ugly. They're beautiful. Oh, phooey, it's just the lighting, I told myself firmly, and put on my shirt. I half ran back up the long beach to the house. It was even farther than I thought it was, and I crept into my room quietly, stripped, put on a nightgown and went straight to sleep.

That night, I had a dream. It was so startlingly vivid, it frightened me. I forgot most of it as soon as I woke up, but the end of it stayed with me, coming to me again and again all day. Chloe was kissing me on the lips.

I had to talk to her; I couldn't put it off anymore. I waited till late afternoon, and when Lilli was napping and the others were out at the beach I called her house. There was no answer. I got the number of Mr. Fox's law firm and they gave me a number in Connecticut where I could reach her. I thanked them, and dialed the number they'd given me. I held my breath, and Chloe answered the phone.

"Chloe?" I said hesitantly.

"Val?"

"Chloe?"

"Val!"

"Oh, Chloe—Chloe, I had to call you, I got your number from someone at the firm—is it O.K.?"

"*Yeah*—where *are* you?"

"In Amagansett," I said, as though I were saying "Japan." "I'm quitting. I'll be home tomorrow. What are you doing in Connecticut?"

"I told you I'd be here, remember? Mom rented a house. Should you be calling me long distance?"

"You're damn right I should. Aren't you glad to talk to me?"

"Yes! Of course I am!"

"Chloe, I had a really weird dream about you. I'm almost afraid to tell you."

"Don't be afraid. What was it? Did you murder me?"

"No," I said, shifting uncomfortably. "Chloe, I have to talk to you."

She was silent. "Yeah," she said finally. "But not now. When I see you."

"Oh, that's O.K.," I said hurriedly. "Whenever you want."

"Look, I'm going home on Sunday. Will you be in the city?"

"Till the end of next week. My father's picking me up

and we're going to the city instead of straight to Massachusetts."

"O.K., how about Monday?"

"Monday. Sure."

"O.K. Monday then. I'll be over at four o'clock. Look, I've really gotta go. I have to wash my hair."

"Why?" I said suspiciously.

"I'm going to play tennis."

"With a guy?"

"Yeah."

"Oh," I said despondently, and stared off at the wall.

"Val? Don't sound so sad. I'll see you Monday, O.K.? I'm so glad you called. . . ."

My face lifted itself. "I was afraid I'd never see you again," I whispered.

"Oh, sure. Well, you will. Oh—gotta go. *Bye*." I heard a loud smack as she kissed me through the receiver, and hung up.

12

IT WAS sweltering in the city on Monday, but it felt like paradise being free again. I went out for a while in the early afternoon to buy some food, and the sidewalks seemed to shimmer in the heavy, humid summer haze. Before I went home I went into the park and saw all the kids that couldn't go away for the summer running around the playground, with bushed-looking mothers or nannies mopping their foreheads on nearby benches under sickly city trees. Soon I turned back and trudged up the hill with my grocery bag, wondering nervously what Chloe and I would say to each other. Dad was out and wouldn't be home till late, and I was glad. Boy, if he knew what Chloe and I had to talk about, I thought; would he ever be shocked!

I spent the rest of the afternoon in the house, tinkling on the piano, turning the TV set on and off, trying to read magazines, but I couldn't concentrate. At 4:30 the doorbell rang, and I ran to answer it. I flung open the door, and Chloe was standing there wearing white linen pants I'd never seen before and a blue shirt. She had a suntan and looked great. I stared for a moment, thinking how much older she looked than when I'd met her that day in the bathroom, and then I said,

"Hi. Only half an hour late! Congratulations."

She picked up her bags and came toppling in, kissing my cheek.

"Now, don't be catty, Val. I couldn't help it. See, I had to—"

"Don't worry, it's O.K. Come on." We went into my room and Chloe dropped her things and sat down on the radiator by the window. "Want something to eat?" She shook her head no. "You look great. What're you all dressed up for?"

"I'm meeting my mother for dinner downtown." There was an awkward silence, and finally she squealed, "Well, aren't you glad to see me?"

"Christ, I've been wanting to see you ever since—" I stopped, and looked at my feet uncertainly. "How come you never called me after I slept over?"

She gazed at me warily and shrugged. "How come you left before I woke up?"

"Chloe, remember what we—what we were doing—"

She gave a harsh little laugh. "As if I could forget!"

I attempted a smile and failed. "Well, Chloe, I—" I knew I was going to cry. She got down on the floor with me and poked my nose gently.

"Whatsa matter, dollface?"

I hid my face in my hands. "Get away! I'm not a doll, I'm me and I'm awful and I'm sorry!" Two tears squeezed out, and I wiped them away and looked at her. "Chloe, your mother saw us."

"I know."

My head began to spin. How could she know?

"I was awake too. I didn't want you to know. I was—scared. That's why I didn't call."

"You were scared of me," I said, more to myself than to her. So I was right; I had scared her.

"No."

"Of your mother?"

"No, Val—of myself, I guess."

I began fiddling with the fringe on my bedspread. "Did your mother say anything?"

Chloe got up and sat back down on the radiator. "No. Not a word. That's what was so creepy." All this time I'd been worried Mrs. Fox had forbidden her to see me again, and she hadn't even mentioned it! "But you know what she did do?" I raised my eyebrows questioningly. "She found that box with my beautiful-lady collection under my bed and she threw it out."

"She—what? What did she do that for?"

"She said, 'What kind of girl are you?' She made me feel like some sort of pervert for collecting them. She doesn't understand. But she wouldn't have done it if she hadn't seen us. She thinks we—you know," she said haltingly.

"She thinks we made love, doesn't she?" I said acidly. "She must love me now. Christ, she'll never want me over again. Oh, Chloe, can't you tell her it isn't true?" I said, feeling like a hypocrite and hating myself for it the instant I said it.

"And—and what if it were true?" Chloe said defiantly. I could see her lip tremble slightly. "What do you mean?"

"Well—look at all the men and women having sex who don't even like each other, let alone love each other. Isn't that the real sin?"

"Yes," I whispered, holding my chin up. "Yes, that's the sin. And how would your moral mother feel about that?"

"I bet my mother thinks sex is sinful in any case," she said dryly. Then she leaned toward me. "Val, don't you understand? It doesn't matter what she thinks. You're my best friend. When I decide to go to bed with a man I'll be lucky if I'm half as crazy about him as I am about you. I don't have to defend anything! Nothing can change how I feel about you!"

"No?" I said, nastily, wanting to cry.

"No. Because I love you."

"I love you too," I said, wondering why it had never occurred to me.

"You know, sometimes they all make me sick!" Chloe yelled.

Who's "they"? I thought.

"We do something like—what we did once," she faltered. "And then there's a choice; either I'm a lesbian forever or I stop being myself with you. When I don't want either one." I watched her carefully, not saying anything. "I mean—gosh, other people must think about stuff like this."

"Really? Do you really think they do?" I said hopefully.

"Sure they do. They must. But just because you think about something doesn't mean you're guilty of it."

"Guilty!" I pounced. "See? You said 'guilty.' But, Chloe, we didn't just think."

"But we didn't do what my mother thought either. Maybe—maybe I've thought about it," she said, blushing.

"Well—maybe I have too."

"Maybe I've even wished it. Maybe I'll wish it again. But I'll bet if you gave everyone what they wished for, it would turn out it wasn't what they really wanted after all. I just want us to be the way we always were." My ivy plant was making shadows on her face, and I watched her cautiously.

"I know," I said finally. "Chloe? I'm not a—a lesbian," I said. "I'm not anything at all. Some guys turn me on a lot, but I'm not ready to have sex yet. What we did— I mean—I did what I wanted to do. I didn't even think about it first. It just came naturally, because I—" What am I trying to say? I thought helplessly. Why is it coming out so mixed up? "You're my best friend," I said. "And now—you won't be—"

"I will be. I'll always be your friend."

You know what it is? I thought. We're scared of each other. I'm scared that she'll be afraid of me and she's probably thinking the same thing. I wonder if we'd have been scared if her mother never saw. Maybe we'd never have had to admit to each other that any of this had crossed our minds. We could have just gone on being best friends and maybe fantasizing once in a while or being affectionate and pretending that sexual attraction never occurred to us. But Mrs. Fox *had* seen; Chloe had admitted what she felt, and so had I. There was no turning back. How do you separate loving as a friend and sexual love—or do they cross over sometimes?

"It isn't fair," Chloe burst out angrily. "God, I can't believe how hung up we've gotten, just because of my mother!"

"But Chloe, it isn't just because of your mother," I said gently. She jerked her head round to face me, her eyes filled with tears.

"What do we do?" she said.

Chloe—is that you? I thought. Always rebelling and always so certain of what you think—what's happened to you?

"What do we do?" I echoed. "I'll tell you what we do. Do you want to be my friend?"

"Of course, I—"

"Are you sure? You're not afraid, or turned off?"

"Yes, I'm sure."

"O.K. Do you want to be my—my lover?" Am I *saying* this? I thought incredulously. Am I admitting that it's a possibility?

"No," she mouthed inaudibly. "Sometimes I thought I did. I just want us to be friends like we always were, and to think what I want. Like everybody else."

"But," I said, less sure of myself, "I can still kiss you good-bye and stuff—like we always do—" I paused and looked at her bleakly. Is it the world out there making us feel guilty? I thought. Is it the world saying, either you're a lesbian or you're not, with no room for Chloe and me? "I mean, I feel like we don't fit into any slots at all, and they want us to, but we can't," I said. There was that invisible "they" again. Who are "they"? Nobody knows about the feelings we have for each other; nobody is literally trying to force us to choose anything. And then gradually it came to me; "they" must just be us. *We*'re trying to put *ourselves* into slots, and condemning ourselves for not being able to.

"We don't have to fit into any slots," Chloe said. "So let's stop trying."

I moved closer to her and looked up at her face. Suddenly it didn't matter to me anymore whether things were "right" or whether they were "wrong," whether the attraction we felt for each other was "good" or "bad." I'd been looking for some kind of judgment or approval, but when I asked adults like Miss Udry or Mom they didn't know any more than I did. But *I* can decide! I thought. I've been so worried about what other people would think I never asked myself what *I* thought. It isn't wrong, I thought; it isn't bad. Maybe for someone else it would be, but it isn't for me.

"Chloe, that guy you played tennis with—that's just the

beginning. Pretty soon you'll forget all about me," I said flatly.

"Are you nuts?"

"No, it's true. Once my cousin Shirley was supposed to have me sleep over at her apartment, and then at the last minute she told me I'd have to come some other time 'cause she had a date. She said that's the way it is when you get older."

Chloe looked ready to scream. "Well, your cousin is full of shit! I'm *never* going to be like that. Never!"

"Really, Chloe? You mean it?"

"Damn right I mean it. Ooooh, I can't stand people like that. Don't you ever get like that," she said, pointing a finger at me.

"Honey, the day I have that choice I might lose my head," I said jokingly, but she jumped down and took my chin firmly in her hand.

"That's exactly it. People like your stupid cousin think if you say no to someone they won't come back. Well, maybe they *wouldn't*, for *her*. But any guy worth anything will come back for you. You hear me?"

I smiled. "Chloe, I love you."

"You have to promise me you won't turn out that way. Do you swear it?"

"I take a sacred vow. I, Valerie Hoffman, shall never dump my friends on account of some guy. And since you're my only friend," I added, "I swear I shall never dump *you* on account of some guy. Do you swear it too?"

"I swear it."

"O.K., that's settled then."

Chloe stood up and picked up her bags. "Listen, I'm sorry but I have to meet my mother. I'm late already."

"As usual," I chided, walking her into the hall. She stopped at the door and looked at me, and I could detect fear in her eyes. Is she afraid that she might break her word? I thought. Or afraid of getting older and maybe having to fight to keep it? "Chloe? Remember before I said I was sorry about what happened?" She nodded. "I'm not. I'm not sorry about anything."

"Me neither." She paused, and then said "Val? 'Wizard of Oz' is playing at the MOMA day after tomorrow. Will you go with me?"

"Yes," I said, letting her out.

I've had time to think about the Chloe I knew then and all that she meant to me, but it's never been something I could define. One hears of love and there are probably people who could give you a list of reasons why they love another person. There were times I made such mental lists myself and wanted to tell Chloe all my reasons for loving her, but I realized I only wanted to do it to somehow justify what we'd done and the attraction we felt for each other, and that the list wouldn't tell the truth anyway. What we had done was a part of the truth, but only a part; the rest was a feeling too complicated and too strong to explain. It's hard not to sound heavy-handed when I say all of this; I've never tried to explain it to anyone before. I've thought so often about the conversations we had, conversations about Patty, and hip size, about school dances, about the most everyday sort of things, and wondered how I could hear love in them, and whether anyone else would if I told them. As we stared at each other that evening at the door before she left, the feeling was so intense and magnified that I wanted to tell her, and tell her in a way that would last and be with her forever. Comforted only by the sense that she too wanted to tell me something, I searched myself for words, found none, and she stepped into the elevator waving at me and was gone.

I walked slowly into the living room and stood by the window, waiting to see her come out of the building. I saw her appear on the other side of the street and begin walking toward West End Avenue. As though sensing I was watching, she turned and looked up toward my window, saluting. I pressed my hand against the window, and when she was out of sight I walked into my room and sat where she'd been sitting, to watch the sun set over the river. "Hey, dollface," I said aloud. "Whatcha cryin' for? Other things may change, but Chloe and I will never change. Not ever. That's a promise. O.K., dollface?" I flipped on the light and blinked for a moment, letting my eyes adjust, and noticed Chloe had forgotten her *Vogue*. I stood still for a minute, and then grabbed a pair of scissors, thinking: She'll absolutely kill me. And then I began to cut.

DEBORAH HAUTZIG was born in New York City and grew up on the Upper West Side. She was an art major at Carnegie-Mellon University in Pittsburgh before transferring to Sarah Lawrence College. She has always wanted to be a writer and has written—journals, stories, poetry—as long as she can remember. She is also the author of another young adult novel, *Second Star to the Right,* as well as many books for young readers.

Dinah L. Harrow was born in New York City and
... on the ... West Side. She ... graduate of
... with a ... in Philosophy ... and ...
... Master's ... College ... She ...
...
...
...